CASE OF THE RUNAWAY ORANGUTAN

ORIGINAL
PRESS

MYSTERY

The 'CASE OF THE RUNAWAY ORGANGUTAN' - Copyright © 2020-2023 by Oliver Dean Spencer First Edition, Hardcover (Cloth) ISBN: 978-1-989577-12-7, February 2023, Book #3 of the James Cartwright PI NOIR Series

Cover Illustration, Design © 2020-2023 by John Naccarato

Publisher: Original Press, Montreal, Canada.

Hardcover (Cloth) ISBN: 978-1-989577-12-7 / Hardcover (Laminate) ISBN: 978-1-989577-04-2 / Paperback (6x9) ISBN: 978-1-989577-03-5 / E-Book ISBN: 978-1-989577-02-8

Legal Deposit—Bibliothèque et Archives Canada (BAC), Library and Archives Canada

OTHER WORKS BY SPENCER

James Cartwright Series

The Spencer Files (Book 1)
Call of the Nightingale (Book 2)
Case of the Runaway Orangutan (Book 3)

Crime Noir Short Fiction

Tell Me That You Love Me
The Polka Dot Affair
The Spanish Curse
The Final Ring
The Conversation

Devon West Mystery Series

The Crossing (Book 1)

Upcoming 2023-2024

Theory of a Dead Man (Book 4, Cartwright Series)
Fool's Overture (Book 2 -A Devon West Mystery)

CASE OF THE RUNAWAY ORANGUTAN

A JAMES CARTWRIGHT PI NOIR MYSTERY

BOOK THREE

Oliver Dean Spencer

ORIGINAL
PRESS

for my brothers
joseph, frank, and dean

Lasting change is a series of compromises. And compromise is all right, as long your values don't change.

Jane Goodall

CHICAGO

01

HE FELL DOWN HARD—stone-cold dead, next to my feet. It didn't take much—just a pull of the trigger. The way I figured, a bullet always had its way of settling things. It asked no questions. Just did what I was told. And I hadn't planned on resolving my disagreement with the Thin Man that way. But he left me no choice. He pulled his Luger, deciding that one of his .28s was the only way to resolve the issue. Trouble was, he missed. But a .22 from my Colt didn't.

I called Lieutenant Ant over at the 3rd precinct to fill him in on the unfortunate turn of events. I told him where to find me, along with the stiff. I explained how I'd been working on a case involving an embezzler I'd been tracking for a client. How it didn't turn out so good for him. In his usual huff and puff manner, he told me to hold tight and he'd be there in ten. It was more like an hour, plus another two for his relentless questions. But finally, he let me go, satisfied with my side of the story. By the time I got back to my office, I was spent and had planned to head home right after. But in my line of work, nothing was ever straightforward.

I found her seated in my office, her back to me in the chair reserved for potential clients. When it came to new clients, first impressions and a healthy dose of skepticism were always in order. Except, everything about this unexpected visitor was telling me to turn and run. But I couldn't. It may have had something to do with those long, slender, aquiline legs. The way they hung at a precarious and seductive angle from the edge of the wood-backed chair. Or her emerald, green eyes that had me transfixed, the way a tiger to its prey seconds before it's about to pounce.

"Are you James Cartwright, the private investigator," she asked. A hint of a southern drawl coloring her voice.

"I am."

"And how does one go about hiring you?"

"They tell me a story, and if I figure there's something to it, I go from there."

"Very well, Mr. Cartwright—"

"Call me James," I said, cutting in.

"I'd prefer to keep this formal. You know, so there's no misunderstanding," she retorted with a wry smile.

"Of course, Miss...."

"Miss Stonewall," she threw out, not offering up her first name. She was serious about the formality. That was never a good sign. Experience told me she was hiding something—either her actual name or the true reason for her visit. Again, the thought crossed my mind to get out while I still could. But I suffered from two major personality traits. One was curiosity, and the other was women. The combination of the two had gotten me in more hot water than I cared to remember.

"All right, Miss Stonewall," emphasizing her last name, "how can I help you?"

"Well, I'm sure you heard about the orangutan that escaped from the Chicago Zoo last week."

"Sure, it was all over the papers," I said, surprised and wondering what a missing orangutan had to do with me—especially one that escaped from a zoo three-hundred miles away.

"I represent The Mutual Trust Insurance Company. We insured the orangutan," she explained, handing me a business card. I took it, giving it a once over. Her name and contact details were centred on the card in raised black ink. It still didn't mean she was legit.

"So, what's this orangutan worth?" I asked.

"About a hundred thousand."

"Wow. That's one expensive ape."

"Yes, it is," she returned with a faint smile.

"Any idea how and why it escaped?"

"The how, yes. The why, we still have no idea. The primatologist who cares for the orangutan discovered her escape route."

"So, the ape's female?"

"Yes, her name's Samantha or Sam for short. And this wasn't the first time she tried to escape. She was good at it. But in every case, she wouldn't wander far. And she always returned."

"Except this time."

"Exactly. No one's sure why."

"But I still don't get what this has to do with me. I usually take local cases, especially of the homo sapiens variety."

"Sam was last spotted near a local park right here in your city," she said, ignoring my rebuttal.

"That's a hell of a way to travel, even for an ape," I said.

"Agreed. Which got me thinking."

"What? That she was kidnapped?"

"Sure, why not? The zoo would pay a sizable fee to get her back. Sam's from the endangered Sumatran species. Less than eight thousand remain. It'd be an arduous process replacing her. Also, the zoo recently acquired a four-year-old orangutan from the Basel Zoo. They hoped that Sam would act as its surrogate parent. The two seemed to bond well. Then Sam disappeared."

"Where exactly is this Basel Zoo," I asked, exposing my ignorance about zoos and geography.

"In Switzerland, of course," she answered with a smug smile.

"Right. But what if Sam and this youngster didn't bond as well as everyone thought? And Sam hightailed it out of there, hitching a ride on the first train out of Chicago."

"Anything is possible but highly unlikely." A twisted smirk followed her words at such an absurd suggestion.

"Whatever the case, I still don't figure out how I fit into all this. I track people, not animals. Besides, you're not sure if someone took her. It's only one of several possibilities."

"Such as?"

"I'd have to give it some thought."

"This may help change your mind," she said, passing a plain white envelope across the desk toward me. I picked it up and had a peek inside. A quick count told me there were close to five thousand dollars in small bills held up in there. "There's another five once you find Sam," she added.

"I see. But if I were to take this case, I'd prefer payment by check." As I passed the envelope back toward her, I added, "That way, everything stays above board. As you pointed out earlier, there wouldn't be any chance for any misunderstandings."

"I apologize if I've offended you, Mr. Cartwright. But I was under the impression that you preferred this method of payment."

"Oh, yeah. By whom?"

"That's not important," she said, deflecting my question, "but finding Sam is. Will you take the case?"

"Let's just say I'll look into it and let you know."

"That's all I ask," she answered, offering one final intoxicating smile. Then pulling out her checkbook, she wrote me a personal check to replace the five thousand dollars in cash. I couldn't help wondering who suggested paying me off. I'd hold back cashing the check until I could be sure she was on the level. Either way, she'd piqued my curiosity. And once that happened, I was like a mad dog craving a bone—nothing would stop me.

02

MISS STONEWALL had given me the primatologist's contact details in charge of Sam. Her name was Piña Cordell. I contacted her before leaving the office. She was amicable in meeting with me.

The three-hour drive to the Chicago Zoo was uneventful. Once there, I made myself known at the front gates and asked to see her. After a ten-minute wait, she showed.

I pegged her to be in her early thirties, thin, attractive, and intelligent, with an olive skin complexion. But it was her eyes that caught my attention. They were full of light and optimism, a rare sighting back home in the Motor City.

Her shoulder-length black hair hung furtively across her thin shoulders. She was sporting a dark blue blouse accented by floral patterns tucked into her jeans.

"Hi. You must be Mr. Cartwright," she said as she walked toward me with her hand extended.

"Please, call me James," taking her slender hand into mine. By her expression, I assumed I had gripped it too hard. "Sorry," I said, apologizing.

"You have quite the handshake, James," offering a playful smile with her words.

"Comes with the territory," I said, sounding foolish. I found myself nervous around her.

"So, how can I help in locating Sam?"

"Well…" I started, trying to regain composure. "Miss Stonewall told me this wasn't the first time Sam escaped."

"That's correct."

"But this is a first for her not coming back."

"Yes."

"What's so different about this time? Did the baby chimp have something to do with it?"

"It's a baby orangutan," she corrected me, "and they're very different from chimpanzees."

"Yeah, I kinda knew that."

"His name is Ombak," offering an understanding smile. "It derives from the Malay word, which means waves. Come, let me introduce him to you."

We made our way through the zoo's inner sanctum—a maze of enclosures that housed its inhabitants. On the way, we passed a proud of lions, a pair of zebras, and a giraffe—which I thought was sticking its neck out a bit too far. A peacock also flashed its brilliant plume, hoping to attract a mate. I wasn't sure if his interest was in Piña or me. Finally, we came to our intended destination.

Ombak was on his back, having tucked himself away in the corner, most likely sleeping. Our approach had awakened him. He moved to the center of his enclosure to check us out. His fur was bright orange, and he had a pair of the longest arms I'd ever seen.

"He's adorable, in an orangutan kind of way," I said.

"What? As in a face only a mother could love?" she teased.

"Yeah. Something along those lines." I replied, figuring I should probably be more careful with my remarks about her orangutans. She seemed very fond of them. And figured she did like his looks. Noticing my expression, she broke out into light laughter. I followed suit. Once the moment passed, I got back to the matter at hand.

"So, what were you saying about how Sam escaped?"

"Orangutans are intelligent and quite clever. I'm not sure how much you know about them," she asked.

"I must confess, nothing at all. I haven't even seen one up close till now."

"That's a shame. We'd all be better off as a species if we spent even one hour a week with them."

"That may be true, but I could think of a few other things to help straighten this world out."

"What's that?" she asked, intrigued.

"For one, teaching our kids to value life over money."

"How so?"

"The way I figure, the biggest reason for crime usually comes down to greed. Or, to put it another way, a sense of entitlement. We breed this idea into our kids. By the time they're adults, all they've got on their minds is to succeed, at whatever cost."

"Why, you're a romantic, Mr. Cartwright?"

"I wouldn't say that. I see myself more a realist."

"They're the flip side of the same coin."

"Haven't given it much thought." I lied. And for the life of me, I wasn't sure why. Long ago, I concluded I was neither a realist nor a romantic but a hardened cynic—it was the only thing that kept me alive.

"You're wrong about kids today," she said, cutting into my thoughts. "Sure, some grow up believing themselves entitled. But millions live their lives in dire poverty. This is true here in your country."

"My country? What's that supposed to mean? You're not from the States?" I asked, taken by her assertion. She noted my reaction, but it didn't seem to bother her.

"No, I was born in Ecuador. My family moved here when I was twelve. And I've never applied for citizenship. My conscience won't allow it, not until things change."

"Hey, I know we have problems, but so do most other countries," I threw back a bit too defensively.

Part of that concerns my anger over the President's latest policy changes. The guy seemed hell-bent on destroying the country from the inside out.

"Wouldn't being an American citizen allow you opportunities? Such as a secure job, research grants, and being part of the change," I asked.

"Of course, it would. But then again, everything comes at a price, including the added pressure to alter one's scientific findings. But by not committing to any one country, I'm free to follow my spirit and maintain a certain autonomy."

"I appreciate and respect your convictions," I said, wanting to defuse the situation. But if experience has taught me anything, it's one thing to believe and quite another to sustain. An uncomfortable silence followed, which I broke with another question.

"What are your thoughts on Sam's escape?"

"Well…" she went to say, giving me a questioning glance as a mother to a child. I could tell she wanted to discuss things further but decided against it. "What makes orangutans unique are their abilities to conceptualize situations and resolve mathematical puzzles. Unlike other apes, orangutans take time to resolve problems rather than jump right in."

"How's that?"

"Take, for example, those peg board puzzles. You know the ones where you slot different pegs into their proper holes?"

"I always get them confused," I said, attempting a bit of humor.

"Somehow, I doubt that." There was that smile again. At least the coolness I was feeling moments earlier was thawing.

"No, it's true," I teased, "I've never been good with objects, but give me suspects; that's another thing. But as you were saying?"

Before answering, she gave me another of her inquisitive stares, still uncertain what to make of me.

"Well, chimps and gorillas will jam the peg into every prospective slot. More of a trial-and-error approach. Whereas orangutans will sit with each peg and reflect. They'll smell it, play with it, and even rub it against their fur as they glance back and forth from the peg to the board. Then once they resolved the puzzle, they'd slot the peg in the correct hole."

"Really?"

"Yes. Really." The glow of excitement was back in her eyes. "And that's what makes me so angry that Sam's gone. If something happened to her, it'd be another blow to her species. They are close to extinction, you know. When they're gone, we'll lose a key part of our evolutionary puzzle."

"The insurance lady figures someone may have grabbed her. What's your take on that?"

"It's a strong possibility, but it's strange how it coincides with Ombak's arrival. Sam would never desert him. It goes against her maternal and instinctive nature."

I was about to lecture her on how many times such instincts went sideways when from the corner of my eye, I caught a glint of green light flash momentarily off the straw-lined floor of Ombak's cage.

"Listen, do you mind if I have a peek inside the cage?" I asked.

"Sure, I don't see why not? I'll go in first and comfort Ombak while you do your thing," offering a conspiratorial smile.

She made her way to the baby orangutan, whispering comforting words. It worked. Ombak immediately moved toward her. That wasn't the case when I entered. Ombak's bright suspect eyes locked onto my every move. Piña, seeing his reaction, motioned me to come toward them. She then asked me to hold out my palm. I did as she asked. Ombak brought his palm towards mine, sliding it over and cocking his head to one side, and giving my face a once over. He seemed satisfied that I didn't present any danger. Or he figured my ugly mug was also one only a mother could love. Either way, he turned his attention back to Piña.

I moved to where I had spotted the reflection. I pulled back several strands of straw, revealing a small object. Grasping it between my index finger and thumb, I brought it to eye level to have a closer look. If I didn't know any better, it looked like a diamond. I wasn't an expert on such matters, but judging from its brilliance and clarity, the item could be worth a bundle.

03

ONCE BOTH PIÑA and I were back outside the cage, I showed her what I'd found.

"Wow. Do you think it's real? And how did it get here?"

"I'll have an expert look at it, but my gut's telling me it's the genuine article. Your guess is as good as mine regarding how it got there. But I have some theories."

"Such as?"

"First, let me ask you. When did Ombak arrive?"

"About a week ago."

"And Sam disappeared just after. Right?"

"Yes. What are you getting at, James? That this diamond has something to do with her disappearance?"

"The timeline fits."

"But I still don't see how this has to do with Sam's disappearance."

"The insurance lady said that Ombak came from the Basel Zoo," I said, pressing on.

"Yes."

"And what protocols are at play with such transfers?"

"Well, the usual stuff. Documents such as a chain of custody, certification of the animal's health and—"

"What about accessories?" I asked, cutting her off.

"What do you mean?"

"I'm not sure about orangutans, but we humans need shoes and clothing. But we also require comfort to get us through tough times."

"Depends on who you ask about needing clothes," she answered, throwing a playful grin. "But yes, Ombak had a large stuffed pink pig he'd cuddle and fall asleep with."

"Next, you'll tell me his favorite group was Pink Floyd."

"You're into your pop culture, James."

"Sure. Who doesn't know about that humongous pink pig that the band floated around during their gigs? Besides, some of my best friends are pigs, having been one myself," I said. "Anyway, I try to keep with the latest fads, though jazz—Coltrane and Miles are more my cup of tea.

"I'm more of a classical gal. Bach, Bartok and Beethoven," she volleyed back with one of her intoxicating radiant smiles. But beneath the smile, her thoughts were on something else.

"Why did you leave the police force?" she asked.

"That's a long story for another day." It came out sounding a bit too harsh. She had dropped her smile.

"Listen, I'm sorry, Miss Cordell, but—"

"Piña, please."

"Piña. I didn't mean for that to come out as it did. My past triggers the worst in me, so I keep my head in the present."

"I understand," she said, looking back at Ombak, who was checking us out. I wonder what he made of us humans with all our quirks. "The pig's not here. It's always with him. I've no idea where it's gotten to."

"When was the last time you remember seeing Ombak with it?"

"A few days back. About the time Sam went missing. What are you thinking?" she asked, returning her attention to me. "That someone smuggled the diamond inside the pig?"

"Yeah, makes sense. But not only one diamond. It wouldn't have been worth all the effort. I figure there's a lot more where this came from. And it would have cost a pretty penny to pull this off, such as paying off the right people."

"So now what?"

"So, now I go looking for a stuffed pig. Hopefully, that will also lead us to Sam."

04

THE WAY I FIGURED, whoever smuggled the gems inside the pig, came back to retrieve their prized possessions. But what they hadn't gambled on was Sam. Suppose orangutans were as intelligent as Piña claimed. In that case, Sam must have realized her late-night visitor wasn't kosher—especially if they were after Ombak's toy.

Piña also told me that orangutans were naturally shy and gentle. But if push came to shove, that was something else. Therefore, another possibility existed. Sam knew the intruder but was suspicious of her late-night visitor. Once the intruder made their move, trying to grab the pig from the youngster, Sam reacted. A struggle probably ensued, causing the pig to rip open, with one of the gems falling out. Perhaps, Sam pursued the intruder.

I turned my attention back to Piña and asked, "Who was in charge of the orangutans the night Sam disappeared?"

"Well, there are two shifts, one during the day, one in the late afternoon and one at night."

"I assume you work days."

"Why, yes. Unless there is some emergency."

"What time did you find out about Sam's escape?"

"Around seven in the morning."

"Why so late?"

"It's when the day crew starts, and it's when they noticed Sam missing."

"Are you saying the night shift had no idea of Sam's disappearance?"

"I guess not," she answered, puzzled by this insight. Then realizing where I was going with the question, added, "That means Sam must have disappeared sometime after six that morning. The night shift makes their last round then." "What about security?" I asked.

"There's only one guard, a retired gentleman who works at the gate and does a sweep of the grounds once every two hours. His last inspection would have also been around six. And we have cameras stationed at all the animal's habitats, which the guard can access."

"And the guard and crew reported nothing unusual."

"No. The police and Miss Stonewall questioned the night shift crew and the guard. Again, nothing."

"Well, they must have missed something since. This smells like an inside job. Whoever was in on this must have known the place's layout and how to circumvent the cameras."

"That's what the police thought, but everyone checked out."

"Can you get me a list of those working the night shift?"

"Of course. And can you keep me informed of your progress?"

"Sure."

"You promise?"

"Cross my heart," I said, lying with a sheepish grin.

My obligation was always first to my client. Any details arising from the investigation were theirs to do with what they wanted. Providing they were legit. If they weren't, I'd shuffle the information off to the local authorities, letting them untangle the mess.

But there were always exceptions to my rules. I felt a strong connection to Piña, even in the romantic sense. For the moment, though, she couldn't be one of those exceptions. The way the case was going, everyone was a suspect, including her.

Armed with the guard's and night staff's names, addresses and phone numbers, I went to work. The trouble was; they were scattered throughout the city. So, I gave each of them a call first, ensuring I wasn't wasting my time chasing irrelevant leads.

I got hold of the guard and three of the four workers on the list. They were all cooperative. Nothing struck me untoward about their answers. Their stories all had a similar ring. Each claimed they had seen nothing unusual during the night in question. The first they heard of Sam's disappearance was during their shift change.

But it was another story for the last name on the list: Allan Abner. Piña mentioned that he hadn't been to work for the past few days. When I tried phoning, I got no answer. So, I decided to take a ride and check him out personally.

I parked my caddy a block away from his place on Mercer Avenue. It was a small, split-level bungalow, one of similar models that lined the street. I got out and made my way to the front door.

I noticed his mail had been piling up with a collection of Chicago Tribune scattered on the front lawn. I gave the front door a couple of hard knocks and waited. No answer. I glanced back to the street to see if anyone was around. The coast seemed clear, so I pulled out my lock picks and worked the lock.

Mr. Abner wasn't too concerned about security. His cheap lock gave way in under ten seconds. Entering, I spotted him right off, lying deathly still on his front room floor—a bullet through his heart.

Judging from the smell and lividity of his body, I figured he'd been dead for at least forty-eight to seventy-two hours, about the same time Sam went missing. It seemed to me that Mr. Abner had disagreed with his partners. He became a loose end. I knew I should do my civic duty and call it in—anonymously, of course, but first, I wanted to check things out.

Abner hadn't been too conscientious about where he dumped the remains of his takeout food, discarding it onto the floor, couch, and coffee table—all in varying states of decay. I found it ironic that he was now part of the collection.

I quickly swept the living room, followed by the kitchen and small office space off the hallway, but found nothing. Allan's bedroom was a different story. On his unkempt bed, a pink pig lay on its side. Someone had gutted it. Its white cotton interior scattered all over the bed and floor. A closer look revealed no gems. If they'd been there, they were now long gone.

05

AFTER MAKING my obligatory, anonymous call to the Chicago Police Department, I got on the i95 and headed back to Motor City. Traffic was heavy, and it took over five hours to get back. My office was over at the old Ford Building on the northwest corner of Congress and Griswold Street. The building had plenty of history.

Commissioned back in 1908 by the Edward Ford Plate Company, it stood nineteen stories high in the heart of Motor City's financial district. It took four thousand tons of steel, ten million pounds of cement, three million bricks and fifty thousand feet of sheet glass to complete, designed in the Neo-Classical and Renaissance style by Daniel Burnham, a leading architect at the time.

I took the stairs rather than the elevator up to the third floor—an old superstition of mine. Plus, I needed the workout. Once in, I made for my desk, opened the top drawer, and pulled out the bottle of bourbon I had stashed there. I poured myself three fingers' worth and lit a smoke. It was all about balancing things out after a workout.

Once I had satisfied my carnal cravings, I gave Lieutenant Ant a call. It was late, already nine in the evening, but knowing him, he'd still be at the precinct. Like me, he had nothing better to do on a Friday night. We had a history—and not all good. I met Ant twenty years back when I was a newly minted detective. I was full of idealism and ready to take on the forces of evil. I figured everything came down to a simple matter of right and wrong, and there was no room for any gray. Ant pointed out the errors of my ways.

Ant was already a rising star. The department tasked him as the lead investigator in a case involving a serial killer targeting young male prostitutes. Through a chance meeting at a local cop bar, Ant and I got to talk a bit about the investigation. In my youthful and enthusiastic way, I told him who I thought the perp was, how he targeted his victims, and why. He listened attentively without interruptions, then presented his take on my theory.

"You're forcing the facts to fit the case, Cartwright. They may or may not be right. But life doesn't work that way. Unless we catch the perp in the act, it's all conjecture and circumstantial. Even with an eyewitness, we can never be sure."

"I'll give you that," I said, trying not to sound frustrated. "But it still doesn't change the fact that this perp is guilty."

"No, it doesn't. But we've got to do it the right way—by the book, or he'll walk free." Our brief conversation became the basis of our antagonistic relationship going forward. I heard Ant's gruff voice on the other end of the receiver, bringing me back to the present.

"So, what is it, Cartwright? It's only been a day since your last confession. Or are you calling to break your record? Did someone else bite the dust?"

The other thing about Ant was his uncanny sense of knowing if I was scamming him. So, I played it straight. The truth would sound stranger than any fiction I could concoct. And the way this case was going, that wasn't far from the truth.

"Before I answer that, let me color in some background for you."

"Can't wait. And if I recall, you're not one for staying inside the lines."

"Funny guy," I said, ignoring his barb. "Anyway, I drove across the bay this morning in search of a missing orangutan—"

"A what?" he blurted out, cutting me off.

"An orangutan. You know, the one that's been all over the papers."

"Yeah, I heard something about it. But you? Chasing down an orangutan. That's something. I've known you to spin tall tales, but this is a whopper. Next, you're going to tell me the orangutan did it."

"If you'd stop all your barking, I'll explain," I said, starting to lose my temper.

"Go for it," he fired back, exasperated but ready to listen.

"Well, someone hired me to track it down."

"And did you locate the ape?"

"It's an orangutan, not an ape," I corrected him, echoing Piña's words, but uncertain why.

"Whatever. But did you find it?"

"Not exactly, but the investigation led me to a corpse."

"I knew it. Nothing's ever simple with you."

"There's more. I also stumbled onto a gem."

"What kind of gem?"

"One as green as an avocado. And likely part of a jewel heist.

"So, what's the connection between a missing orangutan, a corpse, and this heist?"

"No idea. That's why I'm calling you."

"I'm touched. What about this corpse?"

"I figured it was an inside job, so I tracked down a staffer."

"And?"

"And I found him lying pretty with a bullet to the heart."

"Did you report it to the authorities?"

"I did," not mentioning I had done so anonymously.

"Sure, you did," he said, not buying it for a minute. "So, why are you telling me all this?"

"Well, I was wondering if you've heard of any gem heists in the last few weeks?"

"None that have come across my desk. But it doesn't mean one hasn't happened."

"Could you check the databases, specifically Interpol? I've got a feeling the heist took place somewhere in Europe."

"How so?"

"It's got to do with a baby orangutan that the Basel Zoo recently shipped to Chicago."

"This keeps getting better by the minute. You've outdone yourself this time. If I didn't know any better, your story is so out there and preposterous that there must be some truth to it."

"Trying to be upfront, keeping you in the loop. That's all."

"Yeah. That would be a first. Alright, I'll look into it. By the way, who'd you talk to at the Chicago police—"

"I'll fill you in later," cutting him off. "I have a call on the other line."

"But you don't have to call wait—"

I slammed the phone down. The last thing I needed was to explain how I'd broken into the suspect's place and left the scene. I grabbed hold of my coat and fedora and headed out. I had a meeting with a pawnbroker who had extensive knowledge of precious gems. Especially those appropriated without the consent of their owners.

06

MEL'S BUY AND SELL was over on 8th and Livingston. I found Mel in his usual spot inside his cage. His polished bald head stared back at me through a row of reinforced steel bars. Hearing the silver-plated bell attached to the top of the entrance door, he looked up. Most likely, he'd already reached for the sawed-off shotgun he kept at arm's reach below the counter.

Mel had seen his share of attempted robberies during his forty years in business. None were successful. Realizing it was me, he drew his hand back and shouted, "Well, look who the cat dragged in. Long time, James."

"Yeah, it's been a while, my friend," I offered in return. "How have you been keeping?"

"Things are good. Both kids are off to college, and the wife is at her sister's. I've got full rein of my domain for at least a week," he said, followed by an enormous grin, large enough to swallow up his pockmarked, leathery face for a moment.

"So, you spend this newfound freedom locked up in your cage?" I said, teasing.

"Yeah, good point. But you know me. This is where I'm happiest. Some lose themselves with the hundred-plus TV channels. Others in social media. And the ones that can afford it play golf or travel. But give me this," making a sweeping gesture with his hand at the accumulated junk stacked around him, "any day of the week, and I'm happier than a pig in shit. But enough about me. What brings you to this neck of the woods?"

I pulled out the plastic sleeve with the diamond inside and passed it to him. "I was hoping you could offer some insight regarding this gem."

His eyes at once lit up at the sight of it. He took the bag handling it like a newborn baby. He slipped the diamond from the sleeve onto a small black velvet cloth. Then using a set of tweezers to clasp the gem, he brought it to eye level. He examined it from various angles, rotating it under the light from a green-shaded banker's lamp. Next, he placed a loupe into the socket of his right eye, allowing his eye's extraocular muscles to take hold.

The loupe functioned as a magnifying glass to ferret imperfections and other telltale signs about the gem's origins.

"So, Mel, what can you tell me?" I finally asked, having lost patience with his overly thorough examination of his newly discovered treasure.

Releasing his eye from the captivity of the loupe, he turned to me and asked in a severe tone, "Where'd you find this?"

"Can't say."

"Can't or won't," he threw back with a knowing smile.

"Amounts to the same thing, don't you think?"

"Always the untrusting flatfoot."

"Can you blame me?"

"No. I'm no different. It's part of our professional deformation. But getting back to the stone. It's exquisite," he said as he laid it back on the cloth. From my vantage point, the gem was indeed striking. It shone like a distant star on fire, about to be devoured by an impending black void.

"What makes it exquisite?" I asked, breaking my trance.

"Well, it's color—the green hue. Next to pink and blue, green diamonds are one of the rarest in the world."

"Oh yeah? And what are they worth?"

"Two years back, a 2.54 carat sold at an auction for around three million."

"That is one hell of a payoff."

"You're not kidding. I'd say this here rock weighs in at around a carat, and whoever misplaced it will want it back. At any cost."

"No doubt. Know of any recent heists that may relate to such a stone?"

"None. But I can ask around."

"That'd be much appreciated, Mel. Listen, I better go, but there's a bottle of Crown Royal coming your way."

"That'd be nice," his face lighting up but for a moment, then adding in an urgent tone, "Be careful, my friend."

"Always," I returned in what I thought was the most confident voice I could muster.

But Mel was right. Whoever was behind the theft of the diamond would stop at nothing for its return.

07

EXITING MEL'S, I spotted the lone stranger right off. He wasn't trying hard to be inconspicuous. Sporting a black suit jacket, a pair of blue jeans, and dark shades, he leaned against my caddy. I wasn't sure what to make of it. Obviously, he wasn't there to ambush me, or he'd have waited for a more opportune place and time. As I approached him, he released himself from the caddy's side door and moved towards me.

"Mr. Cartwright?"

"Depends on who's asking. And don't you know it's impolite to lean against someone's prized possession?"

"Oh, please forgive me," he said, with a thick Italian accent. "I meant no disrespect. I've been waiting for a bit. Beautiful, by the way," flipping his thumb back toward the caddy and flashing a bright smile with his apology, exposing his phosphorus-white teeth. They were in perfect alignment.

"Fair enough. But who are you?"

"My name is Dominic Sangria. I'm with Interpol," handing me one of his cards. I took the card, worked it from front to back, and then turned my attention back to him.

"So, what can I do for Interpol, Mr. Sangria?"

"You're investigating a missing orangutan?" he asked.

"What of it?"

"Well, I believe we may share a mutual interest."

"How's that?"

"It relates to a robbery a few weeks back."

"I see."

"Can I offer to buy you a coffee? Perhaps discuss this in more detail?"

"I'd prefer something stronger."

"But of course."

I led him to a small hole-in-the-wall bar a few blocks from Mel's. We ordered drinks, a double malt whiskey and beer chaser for me and a coffee for him—he said he preferred not to indulge in any stimulants while on duty. I wondered if he realized the irony of his statement—coffee being a stimulant. I downed my double, followed by a hit of lager. My thirst quenched; I got things started.

"Which bureau you stationed out of?"

"Buenos Aires."

"Buenos Aires," I repeated, a bit surprised. "Why isn't the Lyon office handling this?"

"First, let me ask you, what have you uncovered from your investigations?"

"I'm afraid I'm not at liberty to say."

"I understand your reluctance, Mr. Cartwright. So, for expediency, I'll get the ball rolling with what I know, and you can fill in the gaps."

"Depends on what you've got to tell." He paused a beat, trying to size me up, wondering how much to reveal. Finally, he nodded, realizing he had no choice if he needed my help.

"Well, three weeks ago, a vault at the Meridian Bank in Antwerp's diamond district was robbed. The thief walked out with diamonds valued at nearly twenty-eight million dollars."

"Whoa, that's quite of bit of rabbit food. But when you say walked out, what do you mean, exactly?"

"That he walked out the front door."

"How is that possible? You'd figure a bank with that number of gems would have serious security at play."

"They do. About two million dollars worth."

"What then? An inside job?"

"Nothing so mundane. This heist will go down as one of the top ten heists in history," he said, excited by such a possibility.

"You seem to be a fan of this thief."

"Once you hear the story, so will you."

"Enlighten me," I said. Sangria then dove into his story with unabridged enthusiasm.

"Well, an elderly gentleman began frequenting a local bank in Antwerp, introducing himself as a businessman. He told the manager he planned to retire there because of its historic beauty. And that he was looking for a bank to keep his money and valuables safe.

Over a one-year period, the bank employees became familiar with his kind and jolly demeanor. He'd offer them gifts such as chocolates, coffee and danishes.

It became a weekly ritual for him to drop by unexpectedly. He'd spend hours conversing with the tellers, including the bank manager. He'd bring up many topics but never anything related to jewels.

The bank manager came to trust him and issued him a VIP pass. This allowed him unaccompanied access to the vault at all hours of the day."

As Sangria paused to drink his coffee, I threw a wide stupid grin and said, "I've got a pretty good idea where this is heading."

"I thought you might," he said, matching my grin with his own.

"So, when did he strike?" I asked.

"Three weeks to the day. He entered the vault emptying a half dozen security boxes. Then walked right out with no one the wiser."

"But why bring you in," I asked. "Shouldn't Interpol's head office in Lyon be overseeing the case?"

"It turns out that he used a fake Argentinian passport to authenticate his identity. How the fake passport got past the bank's scrutiny has come into question. But it's believed now that he was an Argentinian National. So, they gave me the first crack to unravel the mess."

"What do you know about the suspect so far?"

"We're certain that he's no other than Miguel Fernandez, better known as the Silver Fox."

"The Silver Fox? Why the nickname?"

"Partly due to the color of his hair, but mainly because of his ingenuity and craftiness. We've been after him for over three decades. But nothing concrete, ever stuck. He was also a key player in the Dirty Wars during the 70s—a dark period in Argentine history."

"And what role was that?"

"He was a high-ranking official in a military junta."

"The junta?"

"Yeah, a military coup financed partly by the U.S. and used to promote state-wide terrorism."

"But to what end. Why would the U.S. get involved?"

"For the usual reasons—money, power and control of resources. But it had unintended consequences. What unfolded was horrific. The junta created Death Squads whose sole purpose was to assassinate, repress, torture, and spread terror on political dissidents. Anywhere from nine to thirty thousand Argentinians disappeared during this time."

"Jesus," I blurted out, disgusted at what our species were capable of. And my own country. "So, what do you want from me?" I asked.

"Any information that can help with this case. I noticed that you were visiting a local pawn shop while I was waiting for you."

"Yeah, what about it? And how the hell did you know where to find me while we're at it?" I asked, impressed that he'd been able to track me down.

"As soon as your Lieutenant searched our database for any jewel heists, I contacted him and inquired why. He told me and then where he thought you'd be."

"I sometimes don't give the lieutenant enough credit."

"For the short time I spoke with him, your Lieutenant struck me as quite capable. Someone who knows when to lead and when to let things develop at their own pace."

"Very true. But I'd never tell him that. It would go to his head. But back to you. How did you pull all this off in one day? Last time I checked, Buenos Aires is over five thousand miles from here."

"As it so happens, I was already in Chicago, tracking the whereabouts of the missing orangutan. A Miss Cordell, the primatologist looking after Sam, told me about your visit."

"Wow, you do get around. So, what did she have to say?" I asked, concerned about what she may have told him. Not that she'd have much to tell. But I needed to know where I stood.

"Not much. But she seemed very fond of you."

"I sometimes have that effect on women," I said, joking but sounding like an idiot. I was intrigued, though. Piña hadn't mentioned the gem to him. One possibility was that she didn't trust Sangria. On the other, she was playing the long game and working for the other side. I didn't like the thought of that last scenario. There was even the possibility that this Interpol agent was part of a setup.

"Ok, I've got one last question," I said, giving him a blank stare. "If it jives with all you've told me so far, I'll lay all my cards out on the table."

"You Americans have such a definitive way of expressing yourselves. Everything boils down to black or white."

"Not all of us. And not everything. Not Ant, that's for sure. Many a time, I've wanted to pull out my teeth rather than hear all the bureaucratic shades of gray he demanded I follow."

"Well, I don't know him, so I couldn't say. Maybe he's an exception."

"That's stating the obvious."

"You know, as a kid, I couldn't get enough of film noir," Sangria said, ignoring my last remark. "I loved how the dialogue filtered through the dark, stark imagery. I'd stay up nights, reimagining my ideas for a film I would someday create."

"So, what happened. Why be a cop?"

"One's an illusion; the other's very real. I wanted to catch the bad guys, not only imagine them," he said but quickly brushed aside his confession as an afterthought. "But enough about me. What was that other question you wanted to ask?"

I figured he already knew what was on my mind. I had to admit the guy was growing on me. We shared a kindred spirit and view of the world. But I still wanted to ensure he was on the level, so I asked my question.

"How'd you connect the missing orangutan and the diamond heist?"

"Elementary, my dear Cartwright," he responded with an impish grin. "About a week ago, two men turned up dead in Zurich. They were smugglers and well-known to us. They specialized in exporting stolen artwork and precious gems. Forensics found traces of animal hair follicles and DNA on the two victims, specifically of the orangutan kind.

We then connected that back to the Basel Zoo, which had recently shipped a baby orangutan to Chicago. The rest, you know."

I took out the diamond Mel had examined earlier and placed it on the table between us. As with Mel, his eyes sparkled at the sight of it. I wondered what it was about gems that got such reactions from people.

With Mel and Sangria, their reason was primarily professional. But for others, it was something else.

Our species has always had a fascination for gems. We held such inanimate objects in high esteem, casting spells over our psyche— sometimes enough to kill for. But mainly, gems were ritually used to signify our love and devotion to each other.

"Where did you find this," Sangria asked.

"In the orangutans' straw bedding. I was lucky to spot it. I was standing at the right angle, with the afternoon light hitting it just so."

"And Miss Cordell knew about your find?"

"She did."

"Hmm…" I could see Sangria's wheels turning inside his head, wondering why Piña had left this important detail out. But he didn't ask why. Like Mel, he had fallen into a trance over the jewel. "Amazing," he finally said, "I can't say with a hundred percent certainty, but it seems to match the one from the robbery."

"What makes you think so?"

"Well, for starters, forty-one blue and two rare green diamonds were taken. What are the odds of another green diamond showing up—in an orangutan's cell?"

"High, I'd say. My contact at the pawnshop confirmed this to be authentic. He said it could be worth up to a million bucks."

"More like ten, depending on the collector. He placed the gem back into the sleeve and asked, "Do you know how they're formed and why it has this magical green hue to it?"

"No idea."

"It's all that radiation they absorb as they move up toward the earth's crust."

"What are you telling me? The damn thing's radioactive?"

"No. Not at all. But its process is unique."

"I'll take your word for that, but from here on in, you hold on to the cursed thing. I've no plans to turn into a radioactive creep or superhero. I've got enough to deal with, including smoking and drinking." And to push home my point, I pulled out my smokes, offering up one to him. He declined.

"It always comes down to that two-sided argument with you, right? And grays be damned," he threw back, smiling.

"That about sums it up," I agreed, smiling back, then lit my smoke and inhaled deeply. We both allowed a moment of mutual reflection to unfold. Then breaking it, I said, "There's one more thing you should know."

"What's that?"

"There was an inside man at the Chicago Zoo helping the thieves. Went by the name of Allan Abner."

"Where is he now?"

"Deader than a woodpecker caught in a winter storm. A bullet to the heart."

"That's a shame. Could've given us the break we needed."

"I agree. Plus, he gutted a pink pig."

"A pink pig?" I could tell from his expression that he thought I had lost it.

"Yeah. That's how they smuggled gems in—inside the baby orangutan's favorite toy."

"But no sign of the other diamonds?"

"I'm afraid not."

"So, what's next?" he asked.

"Find the missing orangutan. I figure it's our only lead."

"You know, this case reminds me of an Edgar Allan Poe story."

"Oh, yeah. Which one?"

"The Murders in the Rue Morgue."

"What? You think the orangutan is behind all this?"

"Of course not. I'm speaking metaphorically. I'm saying that the only way to solve this puzzle and catch this Silver Fox is by thinking outside the box, as with Poe's protagonist, Dupin."

"I couldn't agree more. I've been trying to explain that to the Lieutenant for ages. But he always wants to play it by the book."

"There's a place for that as well, my friend."

"Perhaps. Time will tell."

We finished our drinks and promised to stay in touch. Then parted ways.

THE FOX

08

AFTER LEAVING SANGRIA, I headed back to the office. I had a lot to think about. But I didn't get a chance. Miss Stonewall was waiting for me. She had a drink in hand—one I assumed came from my special bottle of double-malt bourbon that I kept hidden in the top drawer of my desk.

I wasn't sure what it was about the private eye profession that made clients think they could walk in like it was their place. Perhaps it had something to do with me not locking the office door. Or they had watched too many detective movies. The private dick in such flicks always found a shadowy figure or a damsel in distress waiting for him. In this situation, I wasn't sure which category she fell into.

"I see you've made yourself at home," I said, trying to sound offended by her intrusion. To tell the truth, I was happy to see her. There was this animal attraction to her I couldn't quite shake.

"I apologize for my forwardness, but I was bored waiting. I remember you offering me a drink the other day, so I helped myself. I hope that was alright." I never recalled doing any such thing.

"Sure. I've never been one to refuse a beautiful woman a drink," I said with a playful smile. I wondered what else she had rummaged through. Anything important, I had locked up in the floor safe and filing cabinet. Still, someone with experience and time could work around that problem.

I made for the bottle of bourbon that now sat on my office desk, along with an empty tumbler. I poured myself two figures worth and said, "Bottoms up." I downed my poison in one go. She followed suit, draining the rest of hers.

"So, what do I owe this unexpected pleasure to, Miss Stonewall? It's only been about eight hours since I last saw you. Contrary to what you've heard, I'm no miracle worker."

"Au contraire, James, I've heard you've been a busy beaver."

"Wow. I've been called a bloodhound, a son-of-a-rascal, a nosy flatfoot, and a few other choice words I'd prefer not to repeat in present company. But a busy beaver, that's a new one for the books."

"Quit being so coy, James. I'm paying you good money for information."

"So, we're on a first-name basis now? And in case you haven't noticed, I haven't cashed your check yet."

"Why not?"

"I'm still not sure what team you're playing for?"

"I thought that was obvious," she volleyed back, glancing down at her outfit to invite me to take another look.

She was dressed to kill and oozing sexual energy. She wore a tight black leather skirt that hugged her body like a snake wanting to shed its skin. Her low-cut silk blouse also left little to the imagination.

She kept crossing her long, slender legs like warning signals at a railway crossing. To ensure I was reading her right, she got up and moved toward me with her empty glass in hand—a sign of what was to follow. I had to stall. I needed to find out what angle she was playing at.

"I thought you said we were to keep our arrangement on a professional level?"

"Did I say that? I guess I had a change of heart since I last saw you." Her ruby red painted lips were now mere inches from mine. "I couldn't get you out of my head, James."

Before I knew it, she moved in for the kill. The kiss lasted close to a minute but felt longer. It was as if time had taken a break from its strenuous duty of keeping us humans on track.

Finally pushing her back, I asked in a wavering voice, "What do you know about the diamonds."

"What diamonds?" My question had caught her off guard, eyeing me with her elusive silver-blue eyes and a look of puzzlement. But she quickly recovered. "Only that they're a girl's best friend," she said, backed by a seductive smile.

"I'm referring to a specific set of diamonds. They were part of a heist in Antwerp a few weeks back. Which coincidentally made their way to the Chicago Zoo via a baby chimp."

"You mean Ombak, the baby orangutan," correcting me. But I couldn't help thinking she was stalling. The sudden shift in body posture confirmed my suspicions. She had also moved back.

"Yeah, that chimp," I fired back hard. "Don't you think it's strange that Sam should disappear days after Ombak's appearance? How are Ombak and the diamond heist connected?"

"I've no idea. This is the first I've heard of these diamonds." I didn't believe her, so I pushed harder.

"Who suggested you come and pay me off in cash?"

"No one. I mean, no one in particular. Your previous clients told me you were the best."

"Like whom?"

"I… well… I don't remember the names… I'd have to—" But she didn't finish her thought.

A look of terror and confusion flashed across her face as she fell hard toward me. I caught her like one does a football—arms outstretched, then pulling back to secure the prize.

The bullet that breached her back had come from a gun equipped with a silencer. The shooter was still holding the Luger that did the killing. He wore a tailored blue silk suit. Next to him stood an elderly gentleman with bleached white hair.

"I must apologize, Mr. Cartwright, for such a rude and dramatic entrance," the one with bleached white hair said, "but she left me no choice." He emphasized his last words by motioning with a tilt of his head toward Miss Stonewall. Looking down at Stonewall, I witnessed the final moments of her life seeping out, staining the back of her blouse—blood red.

"How do you figure," I asked, trying to hold back the anger in my voice. "She hadn't told me anything."

"That's not the point of this gambit, Mr. Cartwright. She was a loose end, plus I needed something to motivate you."

"I thought that's what she was here to do."

"In part, yes. But having thoroughly researched your background, I never thought you'd fall for the oldest trick in the book. Of course, many prominent men have—allowing the skillful seduction of a powerful woman to feed their blind desire. Cleopatra, Delilah, and Marylin Monroe come to mind. But Miss Stonewall was not such a person. Besides, it was not power but greed that motivated her."

"And what? You're different?"

"But, of course," he replied with an air of entitlement.

"I'll take a wild guess and say you're the mastermind behind the Antwerp heist?" I threw back, hoping to stall as I figured out my next move.

"Mastermind? I'm not so vain as to accept such an undeserving compliment. Besides, such terms are best kept for works of fiction. But if you're asking, am I the one behind a well-thought-out plan and its meticulous execution. Then yes, I am he," offering a smug, crooked grin with his words.

I wondered if he knew that he had just contradicted himself. He was chock-full of vanity and egocentric to boot.

"Anyway, Mr. Cartwright," he pushed on, "the theft of the jewels was only a means to an end. The purpose of their appropriation goes beyond one's own petty and meaningless life. We're only cogs in the machine and must do the bidding of a greater ideal."

"Can't wait to hear the rest of your cold-blooded take on morality and life. But before you entertain me with your holier than thou crap, you mind if I lay her to rest," nodding toward Stonewall's limp body, still cradled in my arms.

"But, of course, Mr. Cartwright. But no tricks. As you've seen, my comrade is skilled with his tool."

I wasn't sure which tool he was referring to, but his sidekick clarified the issue by jerking his Luger at me. I carefully lowered Stonewall onto the floor. Her eyes were still staring out at me. I gently closed them with my two fingers.

Funny, I thought, how when I first met her, she demanded our relationship not be personal. But as I laid her corpse on the wood-slate floor, it was one of the most intimate acts one could have with another.

I felt such anger and rage rise inside of me. I wanted to rush the two, no matter the consequences. But my rational side won out. It would in no way help me avenge her demise. I'd only end up joining her in a funeral march.

Getting back up cautiously, I asked, "Now what? You're holding all the cards, Mr...."

"The name's not important, Mr. Cartwright," he said, his arrogant smirk still clinging to his face. "For now, you'll continue searching for the missing orangutan."

"What makes this orangutan so special and worth killing for?" I asked, playing dumb.

"Come, Mr. Cartwright, please don't insult my intelligence. We both know that you met with that pesky Interpol agent earlier today. By now, you must have all pertinent details."

"Let's say that's true," I offered, playing along for the moment, "what I can't figure out is why get me involved. You've spent a lot of time planning and executing the heist. Why come to me? Why not use your vast resources to find your gems?"

"Nothing is ever that simple. Everything was going according to plan. But I hadn't planned on a mother's love for her infant."

"What? As in orangutans?"

"Yes. And then my inside man—"

"That wouldn't be someone by the name of Allan Abner?"

"Excellent, Mr. Cartwright. You are, how should I put it, a fine example of what the human species can achieve when they are resourceful, resolute, and motivated."

"In case you're wondering, I'm already taken."

"That is a pity. But enough of your pandering. Shall we get down to business?"

"By all means. The ball is in your court."

"My proposition is simple. Find the jewels within the next forty-eight hours and deliver them to me."

"How do you know the orangutan has them?"

"It's only logical. My inside man, as you called him, didn't.

Do you have other ideas on the matter?"

"No. None I can think of, off-hand. And if I refuse to help?"

"Well, let's say that her body will find its way to the local authorities. There'll also be incriminating evidence proving your guilt, such as the gun that killed her, plus traces of your DNA. You know the drill. Everything will point to the fact you murdered her in a jealous rage."

"No one is ever going to buy your bullshit story."

But instead of answering me, two armed thugs with matching suits to the one holding the gun entered. They walked over and stationed themselves on either side of me. The goon who shot Stonewall took the Luger he was holding and wiped it clean with a white cloth. He then moved toward me, gripping the Luger's barrel with the same material, demanding I grab the Luger's handle.

Noticing that I wasn't in an obliging mood, he said," Please, Mr. Cartwright, we can do this the easy way or—"

It was a split-second decision, but I figured it was now or never. I dropped back hard with my hands, using the desk behind me as leverage to propel my leg up and into the approaching thug's chest. It caused him to lurch back and loosen his grip on the Luger. Then, swinging to my right, my fist contacted the other thug's chin. But before I could reach for my Colt holstered inside my suit coat, I heard my head crack open.

The room spun out of control, followed by a black void, demanding I succumb to its dominance. I relented.

09

WHEN I FINALLY CAME TO, my head felt like a sledgehammer had massaged it. Stonewall's body was nowhere in sight. A drying pool of black blood lay next to me—a reminder it hadn't been a bad dream.

Grabbing the edge of the desk, I pulled myself back up to my feet. I went around the desk to where the bottle of bourbon had fallen to the floor during the exchange. Thank God I had capped the bottle. None of the precious liquid had spilled out.

Retrieving one of the glass tumblers that had landed several feet from the bottle, I filled it to the rim, throwing its content back in one go. I could feel the blood rush back into my face. I then pulled the crumbled soft pack of smokes from inside my suit jacket. A half dozen smokes had split open, but two remained intact. I lit one and inhaled its fumes like a long-lost lover.

Over six hours had passed since my encounter with the Fox. I had forty-two hours left to get myself out of this mess. I figured the frame-up would go down as follows— dump her body somewhere conspicuous and phone in an anonymous tip. The Luger that now held my fingerprints would somehow make its way into police custody. And, of course, my

DNA would be all over her. My lawyer would argue the evidence was all circumstantial and that I, being an ex-cop and professional PI, would never leave such incriminating evidence behind. But it wouldn't matter. The jury would eat up the jealous lover angle.

The fact I shot her in the back would not bode well. I'd be lucky to get off with a life sentence. I had to come up with a solution—and fast. I couldn't bring Ant into this. Even if he believed my story, knowing him, he'd feel obliged to arrest me.

I had to hand it to the Fox; he pinned me like a pig on a spit roasted to perfection. There was only one person I could trust, given the situation. And that was Elvis. He was an old informant and now a close friend. I grabbed my coat and hat and headed out the door.

I first tried reaching him at his usual haunt over on Bagley and 24th. That's where he usually pawned his Gucci and Rolex knockoffs. But no luck. Next, I went to his place over on Grace and Kennedy. Again, no sign of him. I then remembered it was Friday, and he'd be performing at the Vegas Club.

As usual, the place was packed. If no one told you what to expect, and it was your first time visiting, you'd swear someone had spiked your drink. I counted at least a dozen Elvis impersonators from when I entered to when I found my Elvis. He was my thirteenth sighting. He was sitting at a table tucked away in the corner.

"James," he yelled over, having caught sight of me. I moved to his table and sat down. "It's been a while since you came to one of my gigs."

"Much too long, my friend," I said in agreement. "But you know how it is?"

"Don't sweat it, James," returning a concerned look. "I get it. You gotta do your thing. I'd rather you be doing that than watching me howl like a wounded hound dog." We broke out into light laughter at his self-deprecating comment.

Elvis always had a way of making light of a bad situation. But he had his share of rough times, having grown up on the backstreets of the Motor City. He had to learn fast and hard how to avoid the scythe of the grim reaper.

"Am I to assume you're on some case and you require my invaluable advice," Elvis said with a knowing smile.

"That I am," offering a smile back. "There's some garbage I need taken care of. There's this guy I'm tracking. He's already responsible for four deaths. One was this woman he gunned down in front of me at my office earlier today."

"That's pretty messed up. But why kill her and not you?"

"To make a point. She was in on a heist, then became a liability. In fact, she's the one that hired me in the first place."

"That can't be good for business once word gets out you got a client killed."

"I don't remember Elvis being so funny."

"I'm working on a second career if this gig doesn't pan out. But I still don't get why he let you live. You're a witness."

"He wants to frame me—use it as leverage to find the jewels."

"What jewels? Jesus, James, I have to say, Holmes' got nothing on you. Sure, the guy can be clever with all his deductive skills, but his cases can sometimes border on the mundane. But not yours. It's one blow after another. So, how can I be of service?"

I first ordered a double bourbon and a locally brewed lager for Elvis, which was all the craze now. I then delved into what had unfolded from the time Miss Stonewall walked into my office.

"You gotta be kidding. An orangutan?"

"Yeah, I know."

"This thing is getting more surreal by the minute. It's been said that reality can sometimes be stranger than fiction. You couldn't make this kind of shit up even if you tried."

"So says a forty-year-old man dressed up as a dead pop star," I threw back, ribbing him. "But I have to agree." I added. "what's happened so far is only the tip of the iceberg. My gut tells me this guy is after more than just diamonds. It's what he said about the heist. It not being about greed or money. That's bugging me."

"What else could it be about? He's only messing with your head. Like most psychopaths, they'll say whatever to justify their actions."

"You might be right, but I still can't shake this feeling."

"I hope you didn't come here to ask me to run after some runaway orangutan."

"Why not? It'd be a good workout for you," I teased. Elvis had put on a few pounds over the years, wanting to mimic his idol's later years.

"Look who's talking?" he threw back. And he was right. I had also let myself go.

"No orangutans for you, Elvis. I've got that covered. I need you to keep your ear to the ground and find out if anyone's trying to palm off diamonds. Blue and green ones, to be precise."

"No problem, Jimmy boy. Will do," he said, glancing over at the stage—my fourteenth Elvis sighting just wrapping up their act. "I'm up next, so I got to get ready."

"Sure. Listen, Elvis—"

"I know you can't stay," he said, disappointed but trying to keep it out of his voice.

"Sorry pal, but I've only got about forty hours left to find those gems before—"

"Don't sweat it. There's always another gig. Just be careful, James. This guy sounds nasty."

"Will do."

I ordered one last double before leaving. As I exited the bar, my Elvis had broken into one of Presley's most recognizable tunes, Hound Dog, with the crowd jumping in and singing along… *you ain't nothing but a hound dog, cryin' all the time, well, you ain't never caught a rabbit, and you ain't no friend of mine…*

10

WHEN I GOT BACK TO THE OFFICE, the pool of blood was still there. I could clean it up, destroying evidence—hard, cold evidence that would put me away for a very long time. But I left it, uncertain what my next move should be. Meanwhile, the blinking red light from my post-WWII answering machine alerted me that I had messages.

The first three were from bill collectors, which I fast-forwarded. The fourth was from Lieutenant Ant asking to call back. He didn't sound so happy. The fifth lit me up like the first ray of sunlight pushing through after a thunderstorm. It was Piña. She was in town and wanted to get together. She had left me a number where I could reach her. Ignoring the remaining messages, I dialed the number. She answered on the third ring.

"Hello," I heard the familiar voice say, sounding more like a question than a greeting.

"Hi. It's James Cartwright," I said, trying to be all formal-like but sounding more like a sales rep selling insurance.

"Oh, hello, James," she responded with excitement in her voice. "How are you?"

"Okay," I said, uncertain how to continue, but finally blurted out, "I'm still searching for Sam."

"Good to hear. And that's the reason I'm in town. Your Lieutenant Ant was in touch with me. He wanted to ask more questions about Sam, including the diamond we found."

"What did you tell him?"

"Only that you had it."

Ant was going to be royally pissed for leaving out that minor detail. Likely the reason for his call. He'd lecture me on how I should have turned it over to the local authorities. But he should know better, having intimate knowledge of how I work. I'd argue I did the right thing by handing it over to an Interpol agent.

"I hope I'm not being too forward," Piña asked, cutting off my train of thought. "But I was wondering if we could grab some dinner together."

"That'd be swell," I answered a bit too quickly. And what was up with using the word swell? It made me suddenly feel much older than my fifty-two years. I wondered what she thought, but it didn't faze her.

"Do you have a place in mind?" she asked. But my mind went into a deep freeze. Give me a cold-blooded killer to chase down any day of the week, and I'd have countless ideas on how to do it. But for dating rituals, especially with someone you were sweet on—forget it, I was like a fish out of water.

"Hmm… mm… I, well—what kind of food do you like," I finally asked.

"Pretty well anything, except meat. I'm okay with fish though. And it doesn't have to be anything fancy."

"Okay, that helps. I've got a place. It's a local pub that serves up the best fish n'chips in the state."

"Sounds perfect."

"What time do you want me to pick you up?" I asked.

"I could be ready in an hour."

"An hour it is, then," I said, sounding like a nervous preadolescent on their first date. She gave me her location and then hung up.

What the hell was I doing? I thought. I'm in the middle of an investigation, with four people dead; one of which I was being framed for, and here I was contemplating my romantic future. Humans are a strange breed—never getting our priorities straight. Then again, maybe we were—in terms of our selfish desires making for a messy and painful existence.

The Prince and Pauper was an English-style pub on Rosa Parks Boulevard in Corktown. I went there whenever I got a craving for old-fashioned fish n'chips.

I picked Piña up at the allotted hour. She wore a skirt with subdued flower patterns offset by a button-down black blouse. The blouse emphasized her slender neck that arched down towards her breasts. She'd pulled her hair back into a ponytail, and there was no evidence of makeup on her face. She didn't need any. To my eyes, she was a natural beauty.

We made small talk on the way. I asked why she'd become a primatologist. She said she had wanted to make a difference. Of course, she wanted to know more about me and my work. But in my typical fashion, I fended her off with another question. She caught on fast, so let it go.

Once inside the pub, we took a table in the back. I wanted to be as far away as possible from the onslaught of university students that frequented the place every Friday night. They could be boisterous. We both ordered the fish n'chips special, which came with a side salad. And following Piña's suggestion, I ordered two pints of Guinness.

"You mentioned that you became a primatologist because you wanted to make a change. What kind of change?" I asked.

"For starters, only last month, the Brazilian courts recognized an orangutan named Sandra as the first non-human person.

Imagine what that means?"

"That she'll be eligible to vote in the next election."

"Always the kidder. And always trying to skirt the issues."

"Ouch. That hurts."

"I'm sorry, I didn't mean for that to come out so harsh, James," she said, placing her hand over mine. Her warmth radiated through my whole being, turning my insides into a pool of butter left out on a scorching summer day.

"I'm the one that should apologize. You're right. I'm very guarded. It comes with the job. It takes some doing to trust anyone."

"I understand. I'm the same. That is, with people," she said, offering a fleeting smile.

"But not orangutans?" I asked.

"No. Even though we share ancestral roots with them, they've kept their innocence. They haven't become jaded and bitter."

"So, defining them as humans may not be a good thing." I teased.

"Well, yes, and no," she said, smiling back. "The ruling defines Sandra as a sentient being. She'll have the same rights as any human, to be treated with dignity and respect. But many won't like it. Especially poachers."

"You don't seem to have a very high opinion of us, mortals."

"It's not that, James. It's so frustrating knowing we all have such potential but lose ourselves in our most base desires."

"We can't all be Mother Teresa."

"Of course not. That's not what I meant. And, she wasn't a saint, even though the church says different."

"Exactly. That's my point. I've seen all types, and it always comes down to the same thing. There's this thin imaginary line that we keep crossing—between good and evil."

"Nietzsche. I had no idea you were so versed in contemporary philosophy. You're full of surprises, James."

"What can I say. I've got a lot of time on my hands. I get bored with most literature these days. So, I turned to Nietzsche, Heidegger, and Sartre. They help keep my mind sharp and open to possibilities."

"So, you're not a romantic but an existentialist."

"Guilty as charged."

"I've read little of Nietzsche, but I find it disturbing how the Nazis perverted his ideas."

"You're referring to his idea of *the will to power*, one of his most misunderstood concepts. Nietzsche explains that *the will to power is a monster of energy, without beginning, without end.* And I agree with him. The greater the power, the greater the greed and corruption."

I was getting worked up and could hear it in my voice. So could she.

"I'm sorry, James," squeezing my hand. "I didn't mean for us to get caught up in politics. They say if you want to get through a first date, never talk about religion or politics. And we've breached both subjects within the first five minutes."

"Is that what this is? A date?" I asked, offering up a mischievous grin. "I'm sorry as well for coming off so high and mighty. I—" but cut myself short. I had spotted two of Fox's henchmen who paid me a visit the other night. They had just walked in.

Piña, seeing my expression, asked, "What is it, James? It looks like you've seen a ghost."

She was about to turn, wanting to locate the source of my distraction, but I stopped her, saying. "don't turn around. Keep talking as if everything is normal."

"But why James? What's going on?"

I wondered how much to tell her without putting her in danger. I decided to fill her in with some broad strokes while smiling and pretending to make small talk.

The thugs had sat at the bar and ordered drinks. I figured Fox wanted to send a reminder about our arrangement. Until now, I wasn't sure how much he knew about me or my interest in Piña. But now that he did, she'd be a perfect target to exploit to do his bidding.

After several more minutes of play-acting, I planned our next move. "Listen, Piña, I need you to get up slowly, naturally and head to the women's restroom in the back. But don't go in. Just keep walking, exiting through the service door that leads into the alleyway. Then head to the car and get in."

"Then what?"

"Then wait for me. I'll be right behind you."

"But—"

"Go now," I said, cutting her off. She gave me one last troubled look, then got up and headed for the exit.

I stole a glance toward the two thugs. They had noted Piña's sudden departure but did nothing. They thought she was off to the washroom. It was hard to miss the overhead washroom sign above the passageway.

I called the waitress over and ordered a couple of drinks. I told her it was for my friends sitting at the bar. I then placed enough money on the table to cover the tab, plus a sizable tip. I watched as she delivered the drink, momentarily distracting them. I made for the exit.

Piña was waiting for me in my caddy as instructed. As I pulled out, I caught sight of the two would-be pursuers exiting the alleyway. Spotting us, they made a run for their vehicle. But their objective was futile. I now had the advantage and head start. After ten minutes of winding through side streets, confident that we had lost our tail, I headed back on the i95.

I planned to stash Piña at a small motel on the city's outskirts, run by an acquaintance of mine. Someone I trusted. I explained to Piña that her life was in danger and that I was sorry to have dragged her into all this.

"What's going on, James? What is it you're not telling me?"

"Any other information I have would put you at even greater risk and make you an accomplice after the fact."

"So, your intent is a noble one. To protect me?" her face lighting up with an affectionate but questioning smile.

"I should never have agreed to meet you for dinner. It was like painting a target on your back."

"But I'm glad you took me up on my offer," she said, placing her hand on my leg. Instead of being excited by her words and gestures, I was overwhelmed with dread and confusion. There wasn't any good ending to this story. I'd been here before. Anyone who got too close to me always got hurt. Turning to her, I said, "Me too." I lied.

Finally, we reached our destination. It was a welcoming distraction to my dark thoughts. I parked the caddy and told Piña to sit tight while I checked us in.

"Us?" she asked, adding a playful smile.

"I—I mean, you…." stumbling for words, my face shifting to an apple red.

"For such a tough guy, you turn into marshmallows when it comes to the little things."

"What do you mean?"

"Book me, Danno. Then maybe, I'll tell you."

I gave her a startled and quizzical stare, taken by her reference. The phrase originated with Hawaii Five-O, a sixties TV cop show. The episodes usually ended with Detective Captain McGarrett exclaiming to his fellow detective and sidekick, Danny (Danno) Williams: *"Book 'em, Danno!"*

"I'll hold you to that," I said and exited.

My motel contact, Jerry, was always happy to see me and we spent a few minutes catching up. His wife recently ran off with a traveling sales rep staying at the motel. So, he wasn't feeling that great. I gave him the usual pitch about how things would look better in time. But I wasn't so sure when it came to Jerry. His parents left him the motel when they passed, and by the looks of it, Jerry didn't have much of a social life. He worked at the place 24/7.

Amy, his ex, had been his childhood sweetheart. They'd been together for over twenty-five years. I guess she had decided it was time to move on to greener pastures. But what a traveling salesman could offer her in that department was a mystery.

I asked who owned the red Toyota with the out-of-state license plate—the only car besides mine, parked out front. He grinned hard and said 'it belonged to a traveling sales rep from Iowa.

I got the keys to room 09 and went back out to Piña. She wasn't in the car. I panicked, glancing furiously around. I finally found her standing by the ravine's edge behind the motel.

"Why'd you do that," I said, hearing the anger rising in my voice.

"You took so long, I thought I'd stretch my legs. You're upset with me."

"More like freaking out. Don't you realize how much da—" But she didn't let me finish. She moved in, planting me with an intoxicating kiss. I returned her advances with complete abandonment.

It was around five in the morning before I woke up. I got up to get dressed, hoping not to disturb Piña. But no luck. She sensed my absence. She looked over and asked, "Where you are going so early in the morning?"

"If you recall, there's a maniac on the loose. I need to figure out my next move. But until then, don't go anywhere. There's a small greasy spoon about a quarter of a mile west of here where you can get some grub. Don't call anyone and take the battery out of your cell phone. They may have a way of tracking it. I'll contact you through Jerry, the motel owner, and you could do likewise.

"You're starting to scare me."

"Don't be," I said, trying to reassure her. "I may be all marshmallows for the little things, as you eloquently pointed out last night. But when it comes to tracking down creeps and bringing my wrath down on them, I'm more like Godzilla."

"I had a wonderful time last night, James," ignoring my attempt at humor.

"Me too."

11

LEAVING PIÑA, I headed to Gracie's Diner over on Jefferson, which I'd been frequenting for over ten years. It was my go-to greasy spoon. Gracie, who owned the diner, was a colorful fixture from the neighborhood.

I first met her when she was turning tricks over on Washington. I was the officer on call when she reported a violent run-in with one of her johns that almost cost her her life. We caught the perp, but after that, she made a career change and bought the diner. It was a smooth transition since most of her previous clients, as well as the cops from the 3rd, came out in support.

Her all-day breakfasts were to kill for—if they didn't kill you first. Each breakfast included a heaping helping of bacon and sausages, three eggs, home fries, toast, and a bottomless cup of coffee for $4.99.

After breakfast, I headed to an internet cafe to dig up what I could on the Fox, the heist, and Argentine history. A few articles popped up about Miguel's involvement with the Dirty Wars—how he eluded prosecution and then just disappeared. Seems that his moniker as the Silver Fox was well deserved.

News about the Antwerp heist read more like speculative fiction, shedding nothing new to what Sangria told me. Argentina's dark past was another story, but I didn't have time to rifle through it, so I printed some of the articles to read later. It was already nine by the time I made my way to the 3rd. I had twenty-seven hours left to find the gems.

Ant had a visitor. Special agent Dominic Sangria sat in one of the three wood-back chairs fronting Ant's desk.

"If I knew it would be a family gathering, I would have brought some donuts," I said jokingly.

"You should have anyway," Ant growled back. "You know how my blood sugar gets this early in the morning, especially when you show up."

"James, so nice to see you again," Sangria interjected, trying to ward off the unpleasantries building between Ant and me.

He got up and shook my hand. But it didn't stop Ant from continuing his onslaught.

"Where the hell have you been? I was about to issue a BOLO on you."

"Nice to see you too, Ant. I've been doing some homework."

"Homework? You? That will be the day. More likely, you've been dropping a few more corpses around town."

"Now that you mention it—"

"Mention what?" Ant demanded.

"Well, there's a good chance a body will wash up along the Detroit River in the next day or two." I had decided to fill him in on Stonewall. My newly hatched plan to foil the Fox depended on it.

"Spill it, Cartwright. What gives? Whose body?"

"A Miss Stonewall. She's an insurance agent. She works for—I mean worked for, The Mutual Trust Insurance Company. She's the one that hired me to investigate the orangutan's disappearance."

"And now you're saying she's dead."

"Yep."

Ant gave me one of his schoolmaster stares, trying to figure out what to do next. But from my perspective, he looked more like a mad scientist wanting to dissect me.

"OK, Let's have it," Ant demanded. "Right from the top."

"Well, after leaving Sangria here," I said, nodding in his direction, "I headed back to the office. And who should be waiting for me?"

"Who? We ain't got time for fifty questions, Cartwright," Ant shouted, rising halfway off his chair, ready to leap over his desk to strangle me.

"Stonewall?" Sangria offered up, interjecting.

"Give the man a cigar," I said, imitating the voice of a circus carny as I spun my arm in his direction. Getting no reaction to my spoof, I pushed on. "Anyway, she was all dolled up, ready to put her seductive powers to the test."

"Probably searching for the whereabouts of the gems," Ant pitched in, once again seated, having calmed down a bit.

"That's the funny thing. I asked her about them, but she didn't know what I was talking about."

"Maybe she's a better actor than you thought, or your mind was elsewhere?" Sangria offered.

"Nope. My gut tells me otherwise. Anyway, there I was, using all my charm when she drops dead in my arms."

"Your renowned abilities as a lover are famous throughout Motor City," Ant jived.

"Perhaps," I continued, ignoring his sarcasm, "but the bullet to her back had a more profound effect."

"What happened?" Sangria asked.

"Well, when I looked up, searching for a reason for her demise, I found a thug pointing a Luger at me. Next to him stood an elderly gentleman with a mop of silver-white hair that'd give Mr. Claus a run for his money."

"Are you saying you had the Silver Fox in sight and let him go?" Sangria demanded, not seeming to care much about Stonewall's final moments.

"As if I had a choice." I protested. "I was outmanned and outgunned. Two other thugs walked in minutes later and tried to work me over, but not until I got my two cents in."

"What did he want," Ant asked.

"The short of it—extortion. He wants his diamonds back within forty-eight hours, or he'll pin her murder on me."

"And how does he plan to do that?" Ant asked, still suspicious of my motivations. We both knew I was opening myself to criminal charges, which he could not overlook.

"Well, let's just say there's a Luger with my prints out there and plenty of DNA to make a solid case."

"Leave it to you, Cartwright, to make a bad situation even worse," Ant said, sounding frustrated.

"What can I say? I've learned from the best," I fired back.

"And why didn't you report this to me right off," Ant asked, ignoring my barb.

"For the obvious reason. I needed to develop my next move since I'm not planning on spending the next twenty years in Leavenworth."

"And have you come up with one?" Sangria asked in an even tone.

"Still working on it. But the way I figure, the Fox will do nothing until he gets the goods. In the meantime, we gotta find those jewels."

"And how do you propose to do that?" Ant asked.

"Find Sam, the missing orangutan."

"You've not been able to find her so far. What's changed? "

"I've got a pretty good idea of where she may be."

"I'm listening."

"Piña, the primatologist who looks after Sam, told me she never wanders far. But Miss Stonewall had me believing Sam was spotted somewhere in Motor City."

"And?"

"And I think Sam is still in Chicago. While online earlier this morning, I looked at the terrain around the Zoo. There's a large state park about half a mile away. I figure that may be where Sam is hold up."

"I still don't see how that helps. If the authorities haven't been able to track her, how are you—"

"There's that old saying, I believe, goes something like, *if you can't bring the mountain to Mohammed, bring Mohammed to the mountain.*"

"What the hell are you talking about? You've got it ass backwards," Ant threw back, frustrated with my riddles.

"That's brilliant," Sangria cut in, jumping from his chair. "James suggests we take the baby orangutan out for a stroll in the park. Sam will likely reveal herself to the baby chimp, or the baby will lead us to Sam's hiding spot."

Ant took a minute to consider my suggestion, still holding me with his stare, "I gotta hand it to you, Cartwright, that's not bad. But I also assume you're telling me this because you need something."

"I need you to set this up with the Zoo. You've got the authority. Let me know once you have it arranged, and I'll meet you there. But in the meantime, I have a couple of errands to run."

"Not so fast, Cartwright. I can't just let you walk out of here. You're a material witness to a murder."

"Do you want to catch this bastard responsible for four homicides or play bureaucrat?"

"What four? I only know of two."

"Sangria can fill you in."

"Not so fast, cowboy. What four murders?"

Sangria filled him in on the two smugglers found dead in Zurich. Ant took his time to ponder this latest information and weigh his options. Finally, he said, "OK. I'll let you run those errands on one condition. Sangria is coming with you. I can argue that I released you under his authority. At least I'll know someone as sane as myself is keeping watch over your shenanigans."

"You know I don't play well with authority figures."

"Take it or leave it. The choice is yours."

"Alright, if that's what it takes."

Then I turned to Sangria, who was grinning from ear to ear, and said, "You know what happens to whoever I partner up with?"

"What's that?" he asked, intrigued.

"They end up seriously hurt or dead. Ask the lieutenant if you don't believe me."

"I'm fully aware of your past, James. I'll take my chances."

"OK, then, let's do it. Let's nail this silver-haired son-of-bitch."

We left Ant reflecting on how, once again, he got himself caught up in one of my vexatious schemes.

12

USING SANGRIA'S MOBILE PHONE, I called Elvis to see if he had come up with any leads.

"Elvis, here," he answered on the first ring.

"It's me, Cartwright."

"Hey James, how's the case going?"

"I'll fill you in later. Get anything?"

"Yeah. Right after my gig, I bumped into someone I ran with back in the day. Never guess who it was?"

"No idea. You've run with more idiots than I care to remember."

"You don't have to be so snippy."

"Sorry, Elvis. Just came out of Ant's office. He has that effect on me."

"Say no more. Anyway, it was Ricky the Mole. You know? He runs with the Carmella crime family."

"Yeah. What about him?"

"Well, we grabbed a drink, and he told me how much he loved my performance. After five drinks, he loosened up about a big deal going down—"

"Did it have anything to do with diamonds?"

"He didn't say. But he went on about this pompous South American that Don Carmella was talking to."

"Get a location?"

"No. But Carmella owns a warehouse over on Riverside, 255, to be exact. I'd bet that's where it's going down. He does most of his deals there."

"Thanks, Elvis. I owe you big," and hung up.

Handing the phone back to Sangria, I pulled out from the 3rd and headed to the location Elvis gave me.

Sangria asked, "What was that about?"

"A bit of luck. Got a location of where the Fox may try to pawn the diamonds."

"So, Miguel has the gems?" Sangria asked, confused.

"Not that I'm aware of. That's what makes it even more intriguing."

"And aren't we going to tell Ant what we just discovered?

"Not yet.

"Why not?"

"Because he'd want to raid the place the moment, I told him. And there's more at stake here than catching a slimebag—my neck. Remember, he's got Stonewall's body that could get me hung. Even if we grab him, his goons could make her body magically reappear."

"Oh yeah. That's a good point. Still, we should have a backup."

"I've got all the backup I need," pulling the edge of my suit jacket to the side, exposing my Colt. Judging from the skepticism on his face, he wasn't buying into my tough-guy act.

"You and the Lieutenant have one of the strangest rapports I've ever seen."

"We go back a long way. We may disagree on the approach, but our goals align."

"Which is?"

"Justice."

"Isn't the lady supposed to be blind? And it's not up to us, but a jury of our peers to decide the fate of criminals."

"Funny you should say that. It's something Ant reminded me of when I was a rookie detective. But it's strange to hear you say it. Your country has quite the checkered past with the lady."

"I see you've done your research."

"Part and parcel of who I am. As Michael Corleone once said, *keep your enemies close, your friends even closer*."

"Such cynicism, James. And quoting from the Godfather. That's something. But isn't it supposed to be the other way around—keep your enemies closer?"

"Well, they got it backwards like I told Ant about that other saying. There are always two ways to look at something. For instance, I usually know what my enemy's up to. They carry it on their sleeves. But for our friends, that's another matter. They can flip on you with a toss of a coin. But you're right about the cynicism. It's played havoc on my personal life."

"I see. By the way, are you implying I'm one of those friends?"

"You're still in the gray zone," I said, smiling.

"I thought you didn't buy into the gray zone theory?"

"Did I say that?"

"Not in any exact words, but you implied it."

"Ant must be rubbing off on me. Gotta do something about that."

"And what about Piña?"

"What about her?" I fired back, thrown by his question.

"You're not sure how much to trust her. But if you do and start caring, you lose your objectivity."

"Exactly," I blurted out. "And I broke that rule yesterday. Now she's held up in a fleabag hotel for her protection."

"I see," he said, pausing momentarily to reflect on what I had told him. "But won't we need her help when we take the baby orangutan to the park?"

"Definitely. We'll pick her up once I hear from Ant."

"Do you think it'll work?"

"No idea, but sometimes all you've got is your gut, and a lucky break thrown in, like today."

"I'd say that's true in most cases. Hollywood loves to play up the cleverness of profiling and CSI technology. But based on my experience, cracking a case usually comes down to dumb luck."

"I wouldn't go that far—the part about it being dumb," throwing Sangria a grin. We both broke out laughing.

Once the laughter subsided, though, Sangria became serious. "You know what you said about putting the ones you love in danger."

"What about it?"

"There was someone I cared for. It was when I was trying to infiltrate an extreme right-wing group planning a coup."

"Who was she?"

"She was the mistress of the man we are now searching for."

"What? The Fox?"

"Yes. Her name was Maria. I had inserted myself into Fox's organization as one of his henchmen. From there, I introduced myself, then struck up a relationship. She had been with Miguel since she was fifteen—part of a deal between Miguel and her father. Her family was poor and figured the exchange would give her the best chance of getting out of a bleak future. When I met her, she had just turned twenty-one?"

"So, she'd already been with him for six years?"

"Yes, six sadistic and horrific years. Until she met me, she had no way out."

"So, you promised her protection and a new life for information. But along the way, you fell in love with her."

"I was still naïve enough to believe that truth and justice would prevail. But as you so aptly pointed out earlier, justice has nothing to do with it. It's a dog-eat-dog world, and rules need bending sometimes."

"Whoa. Slow down there, my friend. If I'm reading you right, revenge is never a solution, no matter how justifiable it seems. We must color outside the lines sometimes but keep our morality in check. Or we've got nothing to fall back on. Or we're no better than the ones we try to bust."

"You're probably right, James," he said unconvincingly.

The last thing I needed was someone with revenge on their minds. I'd been there myself, and it clouds your judgment in a big way. It never turns out as one thinks. Someone always ends up dead— usually not the one you intend the bullet for."

"You've got to promise me you'll keep a clear head on this case, or we'll part ways right now," I demanded.

"I'm good, James. If I'd wanted my pound of flesh, he'd be dead already. That would be too easy of an exit for him. I want to see him rot in a cell in Argentina till his last breath."

"Fair enough," I said. "And I guarantee you, we'll nail this bastard before the day is up."

"I hope you're right."

13

I TURNED ONTO the Sherman Street exit off the i95, followed by a left onto Melvin Road, which butted up along the river. I kept on Melvin till I reached a derelict area dotted with a dozen abandoned warehouses. I couldn't believe the area was once the hub of commerce—buzzing with the biggest names in manufacturing. But during the eighties, most companies moved to other countries, taking advantage of cheap labor.

I found the warehouse Elvis told me about and parked the caddy just east of it. Sangria and I got out, walking the rest of the way. I wanted to scope out the exterior first. Good thing we did. We spotted two of Carmela's men in front of the warehouse, engaged in conversation.

"Now what?" Sangria asked.

"Now, we introduce ourselves."

"Just like that?"

"Any better ideas?"

"Not at the top of my head."

"Just follow my lead," I said.

We casually made our way toward the two men. Spotting us, they moved to confront us. The taller and beefier of the two spoke first.

"Can I help you?"

"We're with the new safety commission recently set up by the city to check out all these places," I said, with a sweeping gesture toward the warehouses behind them. As he went to look, I brought my right fist squarely against his jaw, followed by an upper left. He fell to the ground without protest. Meanwhile, Sangria had pulled his gun on the other thug. My Colt was also aimed at the one I had put down. The one still standing demanded, "Do you know who you're fucking with?"

"No. Enlighten us," I threw back.

"This here place belongs to Don Carmella. And you're a dead man."

"Perhaps, but before I meet my maker, can you answer a few questions?"

"Go fuck yourself."

"Have it your way."

We marched the two in behind one of the freight containers. They both eyed us anxiously, figuring it was all over. But luckily for them, I was in a good mood. We tied their hands behind their backs and taped their mouths with duct tape. Satisfied they were secure, we worked our way toward the warehouse's entrance.

With Sangria's back to the wall, I gave a quick hard pull of the door. It gave way without a struggle. Sangria pushed through first, his gun outstretched. He did a broad sweep of the warehouse's interior. I followed suit, also scanning for any signs of life. But the place looked abandoned.

Diffused light from overhead umbrella lamps suspended from the corrugated steel roof above exposed countless rows of wooden crates stacked on either side of us. I had no idea what they held, but if I were to guess, I'd say an extensive collection of contraband and smuggled goods.

But before I could verify my suspicions, the sound of grinding gears from the other end of the warehouse caught our attention. A large overhead door rose as two vehicles made their way in. One was a long-bodied black Cadillac, the other a black BMW SUV. They stopped midway in. We stashed ourselves behind some crates and hoped to be within earshot of what was unfolding.

The limo's driver was the first to reveal himself. He stood around six-one with a sturdy build. Another man got out from the front-passenger side, a bit shorter but, like his counterpart, could hold his ground in a fight. The driver then moved to the back-passenger side door and opened it. A squat, overweight man, who I'd guess to be in his late fifties, dressed in a dark, blue-pinned striped suit, exited. He used a gold-tipped, black cane to maneuver and carry his weight. I assumed he was no other than Don Carmella. A moment later, the Silver Fox exited the BMW with his goons— the three I had encountered at my office earlier, one of which had shot Stonewall in cold blood.

Without saying a word, Don Carmella and the Silver Fox shook hands. Both their respective guard dogs stood several feet behind them with their hands positioned over their waists, ready to draw their weapons at a moment's notice.

"It's an honor to meet you, Don Carmella," the Fox said, being the first to speak. "Your nephew sends his regards from Buenos Aires. He told me to tell you he'll be in town in a few weeks and is looking forward to seeing you."

Judging from the furtive glances of Don's two goons, I figured they were wondering what had happened to their two associates. They probably planned to weigh the odds in their favor, but the way it stood, it was a draw.

"Thank you, Miguel. If you see him again before I do, tell him I look forward to his visit."

"Will do," the Fox replied in a jovial tone.

"So, you called this meeting, Miguel. Why? This is very unusual and puts us both at risk."

"I apologize for this inconvenience, Don Carmella, but I've encountered a small problem."

"So, it's true then, about the rumors? You told me your idea to smuggle the stones with the ape couldn't backfire."

"Everything we do has an element of risk, Don Carmella. But I assure you, it's only a momentary setback. I'll have the gems by tomorrow morning. That's why I asked for this meeting, hoping that we can push our schedule back."

Either the Fox was stalling for time or had great faith in my recovery skills. Either way, the Don was not happy with this latest news.

"You know, my godson speaks highly of you. He says you treat him like a son, but there's a limit to what I'm willing to forego."

"Again, it's an unfortunate glitch, but one under control. If you'd be so kind as to extend the exchange time, we'll get what we're after." The Fox's voice sounded strained. I assumed he was not used to asking favors but taking what he wanted.

"Alright, Miguel, you have until tomorrow night to come up with your end of the bargain. After that, I must make other arrangements." Don Carmella expressed these last words in a dry tone. Yet its underlying implications were clear—Fox was dispensable.

Throughout the conversation, I could sense Sangria's growing anxiety. I knew he wanted to confront Miguel. But I had to give him credit. He kept it together. We watched Fox and his goons return to their BMW and exit the warehouse.

One of Don's men turned to him and asked, "What do you think, Boss?"

"I believe we've got a problem. Call Luciano and tell him to meet us back at my home. And where the hell is Ronaldo and Jimmy? Weren't they supposed to be out front guarding the place?"

"Yes, they were," answered one of his men.

"Marco, you stay behind and figure out where they've gotten to. This whole thing is leaving an unpleasant taste in my mouth."

And with that, the driver opened the limo's back door for Don Carmella, who got in without another word. The limo left the same way Fox had, leaving us with Marco to deal with.

We had two options. Either let him roam around until he found his two buddies or let him join his friends. I went with the second choice.

Sangria then called a contact at the FBI and had the three thugs picked up and held as National Security risks. It was the best way to stall the exchange.

When none of the three men returned, Don Carmella would assume the Fox had something to do with it—that he'd been double-crossed.

14

PIÑA WASN'T AT THE HOTEL. Jerry, the owner, told us she'd phoned someone, then grabbed a cab. She told Jerry to tell me she'd be in touch.

"What the fuck," I blurted out at no one in particular.

Jerry further added that she seemed distressed and in a hurry.

"Damn it. That's all I needed on top of everything else—a runaway primatologist."

"So, now what?" Sangria asked.

"You know which cab company picked her up?" I asked Jerry, ignoring Sangria.

"Yeah, it was Yellow Cab."

"Get the cab number by any chance?"

"What do you think? I've known you long enough to know you'd want it," offering a sly smile and a self-congratulatory pat on the back.

I grabbed the phone on the counter and dialed the cab company. I got an obliging receptionist who forwarded me to the manager in charge. I introduced myself as Lieutenant Ant from the 3rd and threw in his badge number for good measure. Chances of the manager wanting to verify my identity were low. I'd learned from earlier encounters it all had to do with delivery—how urgent and authoritarian you came across. Moments later, I had the address where Piña had been dropped off.

"Okay. Let's go," I said, dropping the phone back into its cradle and moving toward the door. "And thanks, Jerry. I owe you."

"Anytime, James."

The address Piña gave the cab driver was in a derelict district of Motor City, attached to a two-story brick home which had seen better days—its roof having collapsed from disrepair over the years and its front lawn overgrown with weeds.

"This doesn't look good," Sangria said, stating the obvious.

"No kidding."

"You figure the Fox is behind Piña's disappearance?"

"Who else would have a motive. He wanted added insurance that I'd follow through with the gems."

"So, without sounding like a broken record, what's our game plan again?"

"Still go through with Plan A. But Ant will have to manage the baby orangutan on his own."

"He won't be too happy with that."

"I'll be hearing about it till my dying breath. But we've got no choice. We've got other things to do."

"Such as?"

"Well, Plan A always had a Plan B behind it. But I couldn't tell Ant about it."

"Why not."

"It involves meeting up with an old acquaintance of mine that Ant would disapprove of. I figure that even if we found the real gems, there's no way I would hand them over to the Fox. So, my Plan B was to create fake gems to pass off to him."

"That'll never work with Miguel. He'll know right off."

"Probably. But if we play it right and get the Fox to believe I've got them, we can hit him with Plan C."

"Plan C?"

"I haven't gotten all the details ironed out yet," giving Sangria my best, Sylvester the Cat smile.

"I'm all in, though I've not the faintest idea how you're going to pull this off. I've always wondered what it would be like going down in flames while trying to solve one of the biggest cases of my career."

"Don't get your hopes up yet. I'm not planning to recreate the Alamo. But if it makes you feel any better, I'll let you lead the charge when the time comes."

"Well, we've only got eight hours left. I still don't see how this thing will come together."

"Watch and learn, my friend," hoping my words sounded more confident than what I really thought. It was going to take a minor miracle to get all the parts to sync up.

15

I PHONED THE ZOO to listen to my messages and check if any co-workers needed assistance. James would be furious with me, but I was committed to my job and those who relied on me.

Everything seemed in order until the cryptic message from an unknown caller. A voice I didn't recognize demanded I meet him at the address provided if I didn't want any harm to befall my sister. I was not to call anyone, including the cops—I assumed that also meant James.

They said they were watching my every move and would know if I didn't follow instructions. I had no choice but to do as the caller demanded.

The hotel owner Jerry was standing behind the counter when I made the first call. He seemed glued to my every word. So, when I made my second call, I explained to him it was personal. He obliged, making his way into the back room. The cab company told me they'd be there in ten minutes.

Once the cab dropped me off at the prearranged location, I found a young man waiting. He was dressed in a black, double-breasted silk suit. He was standing next to a black BMW SUV. He instructed me to get into the back. I demanded to see my sister first. He told me she was safe if I followed orders. I knew I had no choice but to comply. So, I got in.

Twenty minutes later, we arrived at our intended destination; a low-lying, flat-roof industrial building housing a dozen businesses. The SUV drove around back, stopping in front of a loading dock that led to one of the units. And, as if on cue, the unit's door opened. A cloned individual matching the driver made his way to the car. Before opening my door, he scanned the area, ensuring the coast was clear. Satisfied, he opened it, peered in, and asked politely, "Miss Cordell?"

"Yes."

"Could you please follow me? Mr. Fernandez would like a moment of your time."

How absurd, I thought, as if I could refuse. And what if I did? Would they release my sister, drive me back home and forget that the whole thing happened? Not a chance in hell. So, I got out and followed the stranger.

An older gentleman with a mop of silver-white hair was seated behind a finely polished mahogany desk. He immediately got up when he saw me and approached me.

"Such a pleasure to meet you," he said enthusiastically, extending his hand. "I've heard such great things about you. The work you've done with orangutans is commendable."

"Why have you brought me here? And where's my sister? I want to see her now!" I demanded, ignoring his extended hand and compliments.

"I understand you're confused and upset by what's happened. But let me assure you that your sister is fine. Call her and find out for yourself," and gestured to one of his men to give me their mobile phone. I grabbed it with my shaking hands and dialed my sister's number. She picked up on the second ring.

"Sis? Are you okay?"

"Sure. Why wouldn't I be? What's going on? Why are you asking me? And what number are you calling from? It's blocked. I almost didn't pick up—"

"Where are you now?" I asked, cutting her off. Of course, I knew exactly where she was since I dialed her home number. But still, I wanted confirmation.

"At home with the kids. Piña. You're scaring me."

"It's nothing, sis. Just had a bad dream."

"What? At two in the afternoon?"

"I'll explain later. Gotta go," I said and hung up.

"See," the silver-haired man said, "all is fine, providing you do exactly as I say."

"Which is?"

"Well, for starters, let's make one more phone call together, shall we," extending his open palm toward me. I passed the phone over.

"And let's put it on speakerphone, so we all can hear," he said. Then dialed a number.

"Sangria, here."

"Well, hello, Angelo. So nice to hear your voice again."

"Miguel?"

"I assume Mr. Cartwright is with you."

"What of it?" Sangria said, turning to Cartwright and putting Miguel on speaker.

"I would have called Cartwright directly on this matter. But seeing that he refuses to embrace the wonders of modern technology, he left me little choice. I know it must not be pleasant to hear my voice, given our past."

"Cut with your gentleman's facade. We both know what you are. Get to the point." Sangria fired back.

"You haven't changed your rude and crude behavior a bit. I never understood what Maria saw in you."

"Listen, you son-of-a-bit—"

But Cartwright grabbed the phone before Sangria could finish.

"Cartwright here." Cartwright figured antagonizing the Fox wouldn't get them any closer to a solution. "You have my full attention. What is it you want?"

"The same thing as when we first met, Mr. Cartwright. My property."

"You know you've got that backwards? It's not yours to have."

"A minor technicality, Mr. Cartwright. Either way, I want the gems back, and you only have a few hours left."

"I'm working on it."

"I'm sure you are. But I've decided an extra push was in order just in case the other matter wasn't motivating you enough."

"James." It was Piña.

"Are you okay?" Cartwright asked.

"Yes, I'm so sorry for not listening, but—"

"Ah, so sweet to hear the chirps of you two lovebirds," Miguel cut back in. "You have until five to bring me what I need."

"Listen, you bast—," Cartwright went to say, having also lost his composure. But Miguel had hung up.

16

SANGRIA'S BRIEF conversation with the Fox shook him. I wasn't faring much better. The guy had a way of getting under one's skin. Thankfully, we arrived at our destination, leaving no time to ponder the matter further.

It was the home of one of the greatest forgers of my time, a guy by the name of Martin Lefauve. I met him during my time on the force. Martin helped crack several cases for me as an unofficial advisor. He also served ten years at Carson City Correctional for a botched fraud case involving forged antiques. But it wasn't his handy work that caused the gig to go sideways. It was the amateurish attempt by one of his associates to pass the goods off to an undercover agent.

I gave the door knocker three hard hits. Moments later, I heard a half dozen deadbolts disengage from the other side of the door.

"James, mon Dieu, it has been so long. Ca va?" he said, planting a kiss on either cheek.

It was a thing back in Quebec, where he was from, and continued to be part of his ritual whenever I visited. It always made for an awkward moment since he measured only five feet two, forcing me to bend with him grasping onto my shoulders to accomplish the task.

"Tres bien, mon ami," I answered as he released his grip. "And you?" I asked.

"Can't complain. Getting older. And the body refuses to obey simple demands. But at least the mind remains sharp," he replied in a cheerful voice, pointing his index finger to the side of his head. Then shifting a suspicious glance toward Sangria, he asked, "And who's this?"

"An associate helping me on a case. Which is why we're—"

"Smells like a cop—Interpol, to be exact," he threw back.

"How could you possibly know that?" Sangria asked, surprised.

"Call it a professional hunch," he retorted with a wide grin.

Martin was not a fan of cops, the exception being me. I knew Martin kept in touch with some of his old associates. The odds were he heard about the Antwerp heist and, by default, Interpol's involvement.

"I assume you're here about those gems floating around the city at the moment," he said, confirming my suspensions.

"Can't get anything past you, Martin?"

"I wouldn't say that. Twenty years ago, you got me good.

Ended up doing time in a damp, cold cell."

"You know I tried to—"

"No, No. Water under the bridge, mon ami," gesturing with his hands as if he possessed a magic wand to erase the past. "If it wasn't for you, I'd still be there and wouldn't have seen my grandchildren grow up. But quit standing out here like a lost puppy. Let me offer you a fine French brandy, none of that cheap stuff you get here. A cousin of mine brought it back from his visit to France."

"I'd appreciate that, Martin."

Once inside, we maneuvered our way through a maze of ungodly artifacts that lined the place from floor to ceiling. To the casual observer, it felt like they'd entered one of the hundreds of flea markets scattered throughout the country. But I knew different. Each item had significance to Martin in terms of its history or as reference material to his work.

Having reached a clearing in his living room, he poured us two fingers' worth of brandy into crystal tumblers. Sangria had graciously declined, which made Martin even more suspicious of his intentions.

Finally, we got down to the business at hand. I explained I needed him to create reproductions of the stolen gems, and he only had two hours to do so. Sangria then passed him the diamond I found in Sam's cage. It took Martin a full ten minutes to examine it from various angles.

Finally, looking up, he said, "Such a fine specimen. Exquisite" He had that familiar look in his eyes I saw earlier in both Mel and Sangria.

"So, what do you think?"

"Impossible, mon ami. Not enough time. Even if there was, the caliber and uniqueness of this gem and the ones stolen would be next to impossible to recreate."

"They don't have to be anywhere near perfect. I just need them to be plausible enough to pass as the stolen gems from a distance. I'm using them as bait to trap a fox."

"A fox, you say?"

"A Silver Fox, to be exact," Sangria pitched in. "His actual name is Miguel Fernandez. Have you heard of him?"

"Fernandez, hmm…" pondering the name. "Does he wear an inordinate quantity of gold ornaments on his fingers and across his chest?"

"Yeah, that's him," Sangria responded excitedly. "He wears them like a lion's mane. Believes it will intimidate anyone who dares challenge his potency."

"Yes. I know who you are speaking of. He's engaged my services before my rehabilitation," offering a wry grin with his answer. "But of course, I am not at liberty to disclose my work for him." Then turning to me with a solemn expression, said, "James, you must be careful with this individual. His reputation precedes him. He's dangerous and vindictive."

"I appreciate your concern, Martin. But you also know that no two-bit thug will get the upper hand on me. Plus, he's kidnapped someone I care about, which makes this very personal."

"I see," Martin said, contemplating what I had told him. "Well, I guess I could conjure something up, even given the short time. But as soon as this Fox, as you call him, gets a close look, the gig will be over."

"All I need to do is lure him in. If he gets that close, then my plan has failed."

"Well, I better get to work so that doesn't happen. Do you have images of what the other gems look like?"

"Yes. I have them here on my phone," Sangria said. "I could have them printed if you like."

"No need. Just email them to me. I may be old, but not ignorant," Martin said, annoyed at Sangria's implied innuendo.

"Excellent," Sangria said, ignoring Martin's barb. "What's the address?"

Minutes later, Martin confirmed he had received the photos. Martin said he'd have them ready in two hours and again warned me to be careful when dealing with the Fox. This cautious mantra was getting to me. I thanked Martin, and upon leaving, he planted me with his traditional kisses on each cheek. He ignored Sangria completely.

17

PIÑA DIDN'T KNOW what to make of her captor. He was polite and obliging to her needs. He had ordered a salad, a corned beef sandwich, and a bottle of mineral water for her. He hadn't pressured her with any more questions or threats besides the one she had overheard him utter to James on the phone. But she had no doubts that he would follow through with his objectives. She could see it in his eyes. She'd seen that look in wild animals before, in search of their prey. How they'd move in silence and purpose, following their quarry with stealth procession until the right time presented itself—then pounce, striking the fatal blow.

Two hours had passed before one of the suited men came for her. He led her to a sitting area with a sofa and a large-screen TV set. The silver-haired man looked up from the couch he was sitting on and said, "I wanted you to see this," pointing toward the TV set.

A banner at the bottom of the screen read: BREAKING NEWS FROM THE CHICAGO ZOO.

The broadcaster, a young woman with platinum blond hair, said, "...they found the orangutan that disappeared from the Chicago Zoo. It's been located at a park a half-mile away."

She then explained that the network was cutting to a live feed where Lieutenant Ant of the Detroit Police Force was being interviewed. Ant appeared on the screen seconds later.

A reporter off-screen asked, *"Is it true the missing orangutan has been located?"*

"Yes, it is. The vets are checking her out to ensure she's okay."

"But what does a Lieutenant Detective from Detroit have to do with any of this," the reporter asked, puzzled.

"Well, it connects to another case involving a jewel heist a month earlier in Antwerp. We're working with Interpol on this matter."

"What about these jewels?" the reporter asked. *"Were they recovered as well?"*

"I can't comment on that. But my department will update you once we have more information."

The screen then went black. Fox had switched it off.

"What do you think?" Miguel asked, turning his attention to Piña."

"I'm so relieved."

Miguel, not buying her lie, stared long and hard at her. The asked, "For the beast or yourself?" She didn't answer, so Miguel pushed on. "You don't believe they found the orangutan or the gems?"

"Why would you say that?"

"I can see it in your face and hear it in your voice."

"Well, you're very much mistaken. You'll see."

"That we will." Then turning his attention to one of his underlings, said, "Pedro, get the cars ready. We're heading out."

"Yes, sir." Then left the room.

"You think Miguel bought it?" Sangria asked as we left Pat's Bar.

"Ant did a solid job of promoting the idea. So, I don't see why not? But we'll find out soon enough. He'll want to believe it's true even if he's skeptical."

And as if on cue, Sangria's phone rang. We both stared at it, allowing it to exhaust its ten-ring demand. It was Miguel; I was sure of it, judging by the blocked number. Probably wanting an update.

But I had already decided not to answer when he called. I wanted to shift the game to my advantage. Until now, the Fox had been dictating my every move.

So, we waited in silence for the next five minutes. The phone rang two more times. Once I figured Miguel had stewed long enough, I dialed the number he had given me.

"Damn you, Cartwright. You're playing it close. I'm a man of little patience. Why didn't you pick up when I called?"

"Do you want the gems or not?" I threw back, ignoring him.

"You have them?" he said, excited about getting his hands on them. He had taken the bait.

"Meet me at the old, abandoned Ford Highland Park Plant over on Winchester and Woodward Avenue in an hour," I demanded. "And bring Piña—" and hung up before he could protest.

LA REINA DEL PLATA

18

CARLOS MANDENUS, nephew to Motor City's crime boss, Don Carmella, waited patiently at the Recoleta Cemetery in the Recoleta barrio of Buenos Aires. It was around ten-thirty at night, and Carlos had no idea why Miguel had called the meeting. He didn't even know he was in town. But Miguel was like that sometimes—very secretive about his plans and whereabouts. Miguel phoned Carlos, saying he needed information but wouldn't say what, only that it must be handled discreetly and in person.

So, Carlos reluctantly agreed to meet. But Miguel was already twenty minutes late. Carlos decided to wait for another ten, then leave. *Fuck Miguel and his games*, he thought to himself, frustrated.

Carlos remembered when he first met Miguel. It was at a dinner party hosted by an important Italian diplomat. Miguel oozed with charm, and from the first moment he set eyes on him, he was attracted. Miguel also seemed to know everyone at the party, with everyone vying for his attention.

In many ways, Miguel reminded Carlos of his Uncle, Don Carmella. As a kid, Carlos would watch how people fawned over the Don but also how they feared him.

His Uncle would disappear into the drawing room with his guests during certain events. Carlos eventually discovered these secretive meetings involved the Don bestowing favors on those fortunate enough to get an audience. But such blessings came at a high price, as Carlos later discovered. Once indebted to the family, it was for life. Carlos also learned some of these meets were more sinister and deadly—such as contracting a hit on a competitor or anyone who dared betray the family.

One of many reasons Carlos moved to Buenos Aires was to escape this endless game of death and greed.

He also saw how his friends were seduced by the family's lifestyle and paid a heavy price. And then there was his sexual orientation. It wasn't something his godfather or the family would ever accept.

Nevertheless, he stayed in touch with Don Carmella, remaining on good terms. Carlos even did small favors for his Uncle when asked. In return, the Don took care of him, paying for his college education and setting him up with a decent job.

But Carlos had a gambling problem. Any income he had was quickly depleted. So, when Miguel approached him for a favor in exchange for clearing his gambling debt, Carlos agreed. All he had to do was arrange a meeting with his Uncle. Miguel explained he wanted to discuss an important and lucrative arrangement with his Uncle.

Ten thousand dollars was deposited into Carlos' bank account a day after the introductions. After that, he continued to do other small favors for Miguel. They also become lovers.

Carlos glanced at his gold-plated Rolex, noting it was almost ten to eleven. He'd wait a couple more minutes and then leave. He found it strange that Miguel chose a cemetery for their meeting.

He had never been here before but had heard much about it. It stretched over a fourteen-acre area of the barrio and held over five thousand vaults and mausoleums. It was also the resting place for the rich and famous, including Eva Peron, who had been an iconic part of Argentina's collective consciousness and history. She stood as a symbol of hope and Argentina's spiritual leader.

The mausoleum Carlos stood before belonged to Jose Clemente Paz, an Argentine statesman, diplomat, and journalist. Judging by the mausoleum's elaborate and grandiose design, Paz must have been influential and financially well-off. The mausoleum was constructed of two large white-washed angels carved out of marble resting on their knees in prayer. They were looking up toward a woman above them, also on her knees and in mourning. One of her arms reached down towards the angels while the other grasped at an unlit oil lamp in front of her.

Carlos figured it signified the flame of life that death would inevitably extinguish. Also, a casket just behind the woman, its lid partly opened, exposed a figure trying to escape its confines with a white marble dove having already breached the coffin and was now in mid-flight. A third angel positioned above the casket was reaching down to aid the ascending figure from the sarcophagus. At the same time, the angel's other arm pointed to the sky, revealing the deceased's destination.

Carlos felt a sudden chill. He pulled up the flaps of his raincoat, hoping to warm himself. It was at that moment he noticed a figure approaching. A light fog had descended over the cemetery, making it difficult to see who it was. But whoever it was, it had a long, willowy body that seemed to float, slicing through the fog with a determined and calculated purpose.

Once the stranger was within three feet of Carlos, he asked in a low, growling voice, "Are you Carlos Mandenus?"

"Did Miguel send you?" Carlos asked anxiously in return.

"If you're Carlos, then yes. He has a message for you."

Carlos nodded, affirming he was the one the stranger was looking for. Carlos was still determining what to make of him. As far as he could tell, his pale white face revealed nothing of his motives. His eyes were a deathly ice blue, with his half-smile matching the frozen expression of one of the angels behind him.

"What's the message?" Carlos finally asked.

"First, I need you to confirm something."

"What?"

"Where is Miguel now? It will verify who you are."

"I've no idea. The last I heard, he was with my Uncle. But it now seems he's back in town."

"And who's this Uncle?"

"Don Carmella."

"And where is this Don Carmella now?"

"In Detroit."

"United States?"

"Yeah, where else? So, what's this message he has for me?"

"He sends his regards."

He swore he saw a faint smile cross the stranger's lips. A sharp pain followed, rising from his mid-section. Confused, he looked down, trying to identify the source of his discomfort. The stranger extracted a long sharp blade stained with his blood. The stranger thrust the knife a second and third time into his chest.

"Why?" were the last words Carlos heard himself whisper.

He felt his eyes roll back inside his head as his hands desperately grasped his chest to stop the bleeding. Dropping to his knees, he could now make out the mausoleum above. He caught one last glimpse of the angel pointing toward the heavens. He couldn't help but wonder which direction his soul would take.

19

THE FORD HIGHLAND PARK PLANT spanned an area of over a hundred acres. It's where Ford's famous Model Ts were first manufactured using an assembly line. Because of the Ts success, Ford built other factories throughout the States. In '27, the Plant was retooled to develop tractors but shut its doors in '73. Now abandoned, it made an ideal place for our face-off with the Fox.

I parked the caddy dead center between two large industrial buildings on the roadway. We were about a hundred yards from the Plant's entrance. The stretch of road dead-ended fifty yards behind us. So, there was only one way in or out. The setup reminded me of the old classic Western, *High Noon*.

In the film, a showdown ensues between the sheriff and a rogue gang of outlaws. The sheriff's wife tries to persuade her husband to leave town, fearing for his life. But he turns to her and says, "They're *making me run. I've never run from anybody before.*" Of course, the sheriff prevails.

Regarding our predicament, I hadn't the faintest idea of how it would end, but I was rooting for our side.

"Do you think your plan will work?" Sangria asked, echoing my thoughts as we exited the caddy.

"If I've got Miguel's sociopathic and narcissistic neurosis pegged right, there's only one way this thing plays out," I said. "But in case I'm wrong, run for the hills.

"There are no hills to run to," Sangria threw back with a grin.

"I know," smiling back and acknowledging our precarious situation.

Up ahead, a black BMW SUV followed by two other identical models came into view. The vehicles stopped a hundred feet from where we were. After several moments of intense silence and suspense, the doors to all three cars finally opened—in sync.

The Fox exited the first vehicle, followed by two goons, all dressed in identical black suits. Then, four goons followed suit from the second SUV and four more from the third. The Fox had come with a small army.

I saw Miguel say something to one of his men—probably instructing him to shoot us once he had his precious diamonds. Now moving toward me, I met him halfway, as the sheriff had done with the gang in High Noon.

Sangria wanted to be by my side during the meeting, but I convinced him otherwise. There was too much emotional baggage there. One spark and the whole thing could implode into chaos and death. But it was a moot point since my anger and hatred for the Fox was gaining fast. Now standing only six apart, we sized each other up like gunslingers. I fired the first volley.

"I see you brought your personal army," I said, nodding toward his men in the distance.

"You can never be too careful these days," he retorted with a weak, satirical smile.

"I'm not surprised you have trust issues."

"You gotta be in my business. You can never be too sure." He had missed my point entirely.

"I still have no idea what kind of business you're in. If you're a jewel thief, a kidnapper, or an all-around scum bag."

"Such language, Mr. Cartwright. I thought you were a professional like me. Our transaction should remain civil. Don't you think?"

"Excuse me if I don't share your sentiments. I deal with facts. In your case, the facts speak for themselves."

"You may be right, Mr. Cartwright. Even after millions of years of evolution, the reptilian brain inside us still rules. If we're honest with ourselves, our primal drive for sex and power overrides altruistic intentions."

"Is that what makes you tick?"

"Not quite, though I believe this is true for most people. People like you and I have learned to control such primal urges." I could feel mine starting to rev up.

"I've had enough of your pop psychology. Where's Piña?" I demanded.

"Where are the jewels?" he countered.

"Right here," tapping my side pocket. "But first, Piña."

He gave me a hard stare, trying to pierce my armored face. Unable to get a read, he threw the dice in my favor. He looked back at one of his henchmen and nodded, who nodded to another behind him. The entire process reminded me of an Escher puzzle. Finally, another thug opened the door on the third BMW, and Piña stepped out. She was escorted to me by one of Migel's clones.

"You alright?" I asked Piña.

"I'm OK, James," she said, sounding shaken.

"Now it's your turn, Mr. Cartwright. The diamonds, please."

"Anyone ever tell you you're quite polite for a cold-blooded killer."

"No. Not till now," he answered, becoming visibly irritated. "Quit stalling and hand over the diamonds."

The goon that brought Piña had drawn his gun, pointing it at her.

"One last question before I do that," I said, continuing to stall.

"What's that?"

"How are things between you and Don Carmela?"

"How do you…" he went to say, stopping himself short and regaining his composure. Realizing it was no use bluffing, asked, "What business is it of yours?"

I could see he was trying hard not to let his reptilian self escape. But that was tough, considering I was holding a straight flush. Sangria was now next to me, having ignored my advice. I was glad he did. It could get messy. Fox's other goons had started moving in.

"Enough of your games, Cartwright. Markus, relieve Mr. Cartwright of my property."

"Now, Ant!" Miguel heard me shout, at first confused but quickly realizing the implication of my words. I was wired.

Screaming sirens and screeching tires came flying around the building to our right. I had brought my own personal army to the party. Two cruisers pinned the BMWs from behind while five others screeched and skidded to a stop just behind us. Ant and a dozen other cops scrambled out of their cars, guns drawn, with Ant shouting, "DROP YOUR WEAPONS! DPD."

The goon named Markus made his move as chaos broke, lunging toward us. Sangria acted swiftly, quickly taking him down with one of his fancy Judo flips. Meanwhile, I'd drawn my Colt on Miguel, but the coward he was, shoved Piña into my path. She fell hard to the ground.

Stonewall's limp and bloodied body flashed before me for a second, believing the same fate would befall Piña. My reptilian cortex went into full throttle—my gun aimed and ready to fill Miguel full of lead. If it wasn't for Ant's intervention, the Fox would be lying on the ground next to me—stone cold. Dead.

20

ANT SPENT the better part of the day, trying to break Miguel but with little success. Miguel sat there with a smug smile, never asking for anything, not even an attorney. On those occasions when he chose to speak, he'd dive into nonsensical banter about the weather or how his arthritis was acting up because of the cold American climate.

I couldn't help thinking he was biding his time, waiting for something. But what? I finally convinced Ant to let me have a go at him. He gave me a concerned look but relented. As I entered the integration room, Miguel's face lit up.

"Finally, a friendly face," he said upon seeing me—a stupid, self-conceited grin anchored across his face.

"I'm not your friend," I countered, trying hard not to shove my fist down his throat and wipe that grin away.

"Again, with that American directness, which one could mistake for downright rudeness."

"You don't seem to be in a hurry to get out of here or too concerned with the charges you're facing?" I threw back, ignoring his insult.

"And why should I be? I've done nothing wrong." His arrogance was astounding.

"So why kill four people over nothing?"

"Kill? I killed no one," Miguel returned, feigning indignation. "Do you have proof of such an outrageous accusation?"

"You know I don't."

"That's what I thought. So why am I here?"

"Kidnapping, for starters."

"If you're referring to Miss Cordell, you're very much mistaken. She came of her own free will."

"And why would she do that?"

"I can't say. You'd have to ask her."

I wasn't sure what to make of his last answer. I had to admit it threw me for a loop. But then again, this was Miguel's modus operandi—creating chaos to camouflage his true intent. Shaking off any momentary doubts, I pushed on.

"Where can I find Stonewall's body?"

"Who?"

"You're telling me you never heard of Miss Stonewall? You didn't have her hire me to search for a missing orangutan?"

"Mr. Cartwright. You do have a wonderful imagination."

"And you know nothing about any missing diamonds?"

"Missing Diamonds? Oh yes, I did hear something about that. It was all over the papers."

"I see. And you'll also tell me it's a coincidence that the thief matches your description."

"Yes, I would have to say that is the case."

I slammed a photo of Miguel entering the Antwerp Bank onto the table before him. Picking it up, he surveyed it carefully, even though he was obviously in the image.

"Is that not you?" I demanded.

"Well, it is. Where was that taken?"

"At the Meridian Bank in Antwerp. Where the jewel heist occurred."

"I see," contemplating the photo for another minute. I wasn't sure if he was working out what to say next or admiring himself. Returning the picture to the table, he said, "As you know, they capture all bank customers on video. It's part of their security. And, of course, I've done business there."

"What kind of business?"

"I inquired about securing a safe deposit box."

"Why's that?"

"I had decided to retire in the area."

"Really. Why Antwerp? There must be dozens of other places more suitable for your needs."

"Antwerp has always fascinated me, Mr. Cartwright. Do you know about the name's origin?"

"No. But I'm sure you'll enlighten me."

"Yes. Well, Antwerp derives from a mythical giant named *Droun Antigoon*. He guarded the bridge over the Scheldt River. It's said that the giant would exact a toll on those crossing the bridge. Anyone who refused would have one of their hands severed and thrown into the river."

"That's quite the tale. So, what became of this Antigoon?"

"Slain by a young Roman soldier named *Brabo*, who ironically cut off one of Antigoon's hand, throwing it into the river. Antwerp comes from the Dutch term *Antwerpen*, meaning to throw."

"All very fascinating. So, who would you prefer to be? Antigoon or Brabo?" I asked.

"What a strange question," he said with a smug smile. "But I'd have to say relevant, given our relationship. Or course, you'd identify as Brabo, the protector of truth and justice. Which would make me

Antigoon. But the real question you must ask yourself, Mr. Cartwright, is what toll am I exacting?"

But Ant barged in before I could drill him about his cryptic answer, followed by two Feds.

The taller of the two said, "OK, the interview's over. Come with us, Mr. Fernandez."

"What the fuck is this?" I fired back.

"Let it go, Cartwright," Ant said. "They're from the State Department. Their credentials check out. They have orders to take the suspect back to Washington."

The Fox was grinning from cheek to cheek. I figured he was expecting their arrival all along.

"What are you playing at, Fox? You knew they'd be coming? Didn't you?"

"Now. Now, Mr. Cartwright. Don't take it to heart. It's only a game. And I'm sure we'll get to play again soon."

"OK. Enough of the chitchat," the short, stocky Fed said, taking Fox by the arm and leading him out. I glanced over at Ant, hoping for an explanation. He just shrugged, letting me know he was as much in the dark as I was, and he could do nothing about it.

I was of a different opinion and stormed out.

21

THE ASSASSIN, known as Zero, exited the Recoleta Cemetery. Heavy rain had set in. He hated the rain. The upside was that any DNA evidence still clinging to the corpse would wash away. Not that the authorities would discover any. Zero was meticulous regarding leaving behind evidence, even though he preferred his kills—up close.

Zero had worked for Miguel, off and on, going on forty years. Miguel first recruited him in his teens during Argentina's Dirty Wars, an event triggered through a coup d'état by General Jorge Rafael Videla in '76, backed by US funding.

Videla then initiated state-wide terrorism aided by the Death Squads and the *Alianza Anticomunista Argentina*, or the Triple A as it came to be known. Under Videla, the police and military began arresting and murdering anyone voicing dissent against the regime or sympathetic to the left. Fearing for his family, Zero enlisted in the army to deflect suspicion from his father's left-leaning convictions.

Because of economic hardships, Zero's grandparents immigrated to Argentina in the '30s from Calabria, the southern province of Italy. His grandfather had planned to return someday when things got better. But with the rise of Fascism and Mussolini in the '40s, his grandfather swore never to go back.

So, he planted roots in Buenos Aires and made it their home. His grandfather's convictions filtered down to Zero's father, who passed them on to him. But Zero knew that with the rise of dictators like Videla, his father's vision endangered anyone connected to him. So, to protect his family, he made the ultimate sacrifice. His soul.

Zero had grown weary of his work for the Fox in the last few years. The world was now a different place. No one cared about ideologies and righteous causes. Or so he thought. He believed that, for the most part, it all came down to greed and money. And what motivated Miguel wasn't any different. Even back when he had first met him. Sure, part of Miguel wanted to usher in a new age for Argentina, making it a world superpower someday. But at what cost? And what end? The people would remain poor. Children would still go hungry. And the wealthy would still exploit the precious and limited resources of the country.

Zero's present occupation as a hired gun was just that. He did what he did because he was good at it, and it paid well. And it didn't hurt that deep down, he was a sociopath. He understood this from an early age with his first kill. He had joined the Death Squads at Miguel's encouragement. He was only fifteen.

One day they assigned his squad to be on the lookout for any socialist agitators when they came across two women kissing passionately. The commander in charge asked them several routine questions and then asked for their papers. He then told them they'd have to come with him. The young couple protested, saying they were American citizens and had done nothing wrong. The commander assured them it was just for more routine questions at the station and would then be released.

"And what if we refuse?" the one named Beth demanded in her broken Spanish.

"Well, then we must resort to other means," the commander threatened, pointing the Uzi toward her to emphasize what he meant.

"Let's get this over with," Beth's partner, Karen, said, turning to face her. "It's not a good idea," Beth said, looking fondly into her lover's eyes, considering her plea and wondering if there were other options.

The trip to Argentina had been a last-minute thing. She and Karen had decided they needed an adventure and had heard of the magical nightlife of Argentina. They especially wanted to experience the tango, which originated there in the 1880s. They had even taken courses before leaving.

Beth finally turned to the commander and, trying hard to hold back the tears welling up in her eyes, nodded in the affirmative. Zero and another squad member led them into the back of one of the two jeeps.

The drive took around forty minutes, with the two girls continuously inquiring when they'd be there. But it was once they left the city limits, Zero saw the fear and panic in their eyes. They had become deathly silent and were hugging each other tightly.

It was at that moment, Zero became fascinated by human behavior. There were so many possibilities in how one could react to their predicament. They could try to disarm your capturers by any means possible, attempt an escape, or even plead for their lives. These two, however, seemed to accept their fates. But why? Zero wondered what their lives had been like before this. What their hopes and beliefs had been.

The girls were asked to dig their graves in a secluded wooded area. Once completed, they were raped repeatedly by all six squad members, including Zero. He had initially hesitated, telling the commander he had no experience in such matters. But the commander argued that there was no time like the present to learn.

The girls were then executed with a single shot to the head and thrown into the respective holes they had dug. The commander tasked Zero with filling the unmarked graves. Something broke in Zero that day.

ANTWERP

22

THE VIRUS HAD STARTED slowly. No one was wiser to its existence until it was too late. Hospitals throughout Antwerp had noticed an uptick in flu-like symptoms. They figured it an anomaly, even though it was mid-August and too early for the flu season to be in full swing. Usually, such numbers weren't expected until at least late-November. Thousands were infected, with the virus spreading to neighboring countries.

The World Health Organization, or WHO, as it was usually referred to, had also been slow to act. But once they did, they realized they were on the verge of a pandemic. They began issuing warnings about the virus's spread and its symptoms. They asked people to look for signs such as a rash, a dry cough, watery eyes, or a high fever. And if someone experienced such symptoms to seek immediate medical attention.

The incubation for the virus was anywhere from four days to a week. And half of those infected weren't even showing symptoms. WHO stressed that the virus was benign and for people not to be too concerned. There'd been very few reported deaths related to the virus. WHO also stated they were working hard to identify its origin.

Dr. Emanuel Degas, a renowned Argentinian virologist, knew better. He had developed the virus to Fox's specifications. Emanuel and Miguel had been friends dating back to Argentina's turbulent years. Emanuel, at the time, was a young, naïve, and inspiring scientist. But he still remembered the day Argentina changed him. It all began after President Juan Peron's death, when his third wife, Isabel, took over the presidency.

In the early days, Isabel gave people hope that she could heal Argentina's past. Even the extremists from both sides of the political spectrum began believing in the impossible. But it was short-lived. Twenty-five years of Argentine history, riddled with coup d'états, juntas, and military rule, made for a formidable, if not impossible, task.

Within a year, Argentina was back to its former self. The right-leaning Peron government brought in an Anti-Terrorism Law. They claimed they needed it to fight the increasing violence by the left extremists. The law was also used to erode constitutional rights. But things got even worse. Jose Lopez Rega, who had ties to various nefarious fascistic figures and was an admirer of the occult, started one of the bloodiest periods in Argentine history.

As Minister of Social Welfare, he created the *Argentine Anticommunist Alliance Death Squads*. Between '73 and '76, thirty-thousand Argentines disappeared while in police and military custody.

Some were drugged, loaded onto planes, and dumped into the ocean—death flights as they came to be known. Others tortured in secret camps, then executed—leaving no trace of their existence. Emanuel's seventeen-year-old son, Carmen, had been one such fatality.

Miguel told Emanuel that an extremist left-wing anarchist group called the Montoneros were responsible for his son's death. Emanuel found this hard to believe. The Montoneros usually assassinated political and military figures associated with the Peron government, including the kidnapping of corporate industrialists for ransom. Why would they target his son? His son never associated with any such groups. Miguel explained that the Montoneros had decided on a fresh approach—terrorizing the public. His son had been one such unfortunate.

Emanuel was never the same after his son's death. He left for Italy the following year but swore he'd get his revenge someday. In his mind, that meant every human alive.

Having stormed out of the 3rd after the Feds took Fox, I headed to a local pub on First. It was a local haunt run by Pat Murray, an ex-cop and long-time acquaintance of mine. I'd known him from my days in the force. I sometimes used him as a sounding board when I got frustrated. He stood around six-foot-two, with a solid build. He'd opened the place after being shot during a failed robbery. The shooter had missed the femoral artery in his leg by mere inches, leaving him with a permanent limp and the use of a cane. Instead of taking a desk job, he opened the bar.

"So, you're telling me that the Feds grabbed this Fox guy just like that and didn't say why," Pat said, sounding as frustrated as I felt.

"Yep, that about sums it up."

"Does the Lieutenant have any idea why?"

"Nothing. But he's also pissed. Even his pasty complexion turned a peach red. And that only happens when he's dealing with my shenanigans."

"And you say Interpol's also involved. Wow. You know, Cartwright, nothing ever comes easy for you."

"I couldn't agree more. It's not like I go out of my way looking for this crap. But it has a way of finding me."

"I guess it's just bad karma you're working out. Perhaps an exorcism is in order," Pat kidded, trying to lighten things up. "I know this priest over at St. Mary's who—" but Pat had suddenly cut himself short, grabbing the TV remote and cranking the volume to one of the five large TV screens he had mounted throughout the bar.

'*We interrupt your regular broadcast to bring you this special news bulletin....*'

"Can you believe this shit?" Pat shouted over the broadcast. I turned to see what had gotten him so riled up.

A TV reporter, reporting live from Berlin, sporting a red and brown plaid suit coat and a poorly positioned hairpiece, was saying... '*There have been reports that a virus of still unknown origin has continued to spread. First identified in Belgium, the virus has now spread to Germany, France, and Italy. Reports indicate that the virus may have also reached China, Japan, Canada, Brazil, and the US.*"

"*What can you tell us about this virus and its effects, Jim?*" the commentator at the news desk asked.

"*Well, Arnie, the virus has scientists baffled since there are no serious or adverse effects. Those infected may experience a* rash, a dry cough, watery eyes, or a high fever, which should break after a few days."

"*So, should we be concerned?*"

"*Noone seems to have an answer. The mortality rate has been relatively low. So, until scientists figure what exactly this virus is, they're erring on the side of caution and trying to limit its exposure.*"

"I tell you, it's the end times," Pat said, offering his opinion after muting the volume on the TV.

"I wouldn't go that far, Pat. You know how these viruses show up out of nowhere. Sure, some are more deadly than others," I said, trying to calm his paranoia. Pat was a bit of a conspiracy nut, and I didn't want him going off on one of his tangents. "And besides," I added, "this one doesn't seem too bad."

"You're probably right, James, but still..."

"Strange, though," I cut in.

"In what way?"

"What are the odds that a diamond heist and this virus should originate in the same place?"

"It's what I've been trying to tell you. There's no such thing as coincidences. Most likely, the Illuminati, the Masons or the Pope are behind it."

"The Pope?"

"I know it sounds farfetched, but the church has been behind a lot of nasty stuff. You know that DaVinci used to write his stuff backwards and in code?"

"You've read a few too many Dan Brown books, Pat."

"Oh, yeah. Then how do you explain it?"

"For the moment, I can't. But trust me, Pat, there's always a logical explanation for everything."

Before Pat could counter my argument, the phone rang on the wall behind him.

"Pat's Bar," I heard him say, "How can I help you? Hey, Lieutenant, how are you doing? It's been a while. Yeah, all's good. Cartwright? Yeah. Hold on," passing the phone.

How the hell did he know I was here. Was he having me followed? Or did he plant a tracker on me. I shook my head, realizing I was turning into Pat. But still.

As I put the phone to my ear, Ant let into me, "Cartwright? What are you playing at? Did you forget we had an interview with your girlfriend?"

"Shit. I for—"

"She won't say a damn thing till you get here."

"On my way," I said, hanging up.

23

PIÑA, ARE YOU OK?" She was sitting opposite Ant, her back to me. But at the sound of my voice, she got up, throwing herself into my arms. She was shaking badly.

"Yes. James. I am now."

"What happened?"

"She hasn't been too cooperative. She's been demanding to see you." Ant said, sounding frustrated.

"I'm sorry about that, Lieutenant," Piña said, returning to him. "I needed time to collect my thoughts and to know if James was OK."

I could feel my face turning a few shades of red. The romantic tone of her confession, especially in front of Ant, wasn't good. He'd read all kinds of things into it. Wondering if I wasn't getting too close to the case. The same questions crossed my mind.

"I'm glad you're OK," I said a bit too quickly.

It came out sounding lame. Wanting to diffuse the awkwardness, I pulled away and moved to one of the two available chairs. Sangria was already occupying the middle seat, so I took the one to his right. I could feel Piña's stare piercing the back of my skull. I didn't dare turn around. Finally, she made her way back, sitting in the chair left of Sangria. I wasn't sure how Sangria felt about being stuck in the middle.

Another moment of awkwardness followed, but I finally turned to Piña and said, "Tell us everything that happened right from when you left the hotel."

She gave me an inquiring look, wanting to understand why I had reacted the way I did. Getting no response, she dove in, avoiding further contact with me.

"Well," she began, turning to Ant, "I phoned the zoo to check on my staff and listen to my messages. One message had a voice I didn't recognize, claiming to have taken my sister. He said if I wanted to see her alive again to go to the address he had left."

"So, it was a male voice?" Ant asked.

"Yes."

"Would you recognize the voice if you heard it again?"

"Definitely. But better yet, it should still be on my answering machine."

"We checked," Ant said. "It wasn't."

"Oh my. How could that be?"

"Perhaps Miguel still has an inside man there?" Sangria suggested. Or a woman, thinking to myself.

"OK. After hearing the message, what did you do next?" Ant asked, pushing the interrogation forward.

"I called a cab and went to the address given to me."

"Did you consider calling your sister to see if she was home? I asked, cutting in. 'Maybe the whole thing was some ruse?"

"Well, no. I was in such a state. I guess I panicked and just followed the kidnapper's instructions," she replied, throwing me a *how-could-you-*

think-I-had-something-to-do-with-this look. She was on the verge of tears.

"Do you need a break, Miss Cordell?" Ant offered.

"No. I'm alright. Please continue," trying to recompose herself and returning her attention to Ant.

"You said you called a cab. What happened next?" Ant then asked.

"Once the cab dropped me off, a black SUV shows up. A man in a black silk suit orders me to get in. I was then taken to an industrial unit. Where? I can't say. I was blindfolded."

"Then what? Sangria asked, coaxing her on.

"Well, once inside, Miguel, or the Silver Fox as you like to call him, introduced himself."

"What were your first impressions of him?" I asked.

"He reminded me of someone's father—very cordial and charismatic. If I met him on the street, I'd have never guessed his identity." She relayed all this with her attention still on Ant. As if he had asked the question.

"What about the place? Did anything stand out?" It was Ant now asking.

"The place was small, self-contained, and nondescript. It looked like what one would expect from such industrial units. There were three large rooms, two of which were offices. The third room was a combination of a lunch and dining room with a TV screen. That's where we watched your fake news broadcast," adding a wry smile with her last comment.

"You didn't buy into our little stunt?" I asked, intrigued.

"Not for a moment," still not looking at me. "And neither did Miguel, as far as I could tell."

"So, why go along with the whole charade if that's the case?" Ant asked more to himself.

"That's what's been puzzling me, also," I offered. "This whole thing is playing out like a bad B-Movie. From what I now know about Miguel, he's a pro, but his play since the diamonds' arrival has been sloppy and amateurish. I'm missing something, but I can't quite put my finger on it."

"What do you think, Sangria?" Ant asked. "Do you agree with Cartwright's assessment?"

"I'd have to say yes. I've been tracking the Fox for over eight years, and there's something off with this. He's not following his usual MO."

"What happened after the broadcast?" Ant asked, turning his attention back to Piña.

"They escorted me right back to the room I was being held in."

"Strange," I said.

"What are you thinking?" Sangria asked.

"I'm not sure. It just seems off." And if I did know, I would have kept it to myself. As an ex-cop, I suspected everyone. For the moment, there were too many loose ends to get a handle on the big picture. I didn't know who to trust. Everyone in the room was still a suspect, apart from Ant. I felt terrible thinking of Piña as a suspect. She seemed genuine in her answers. But the questions kept coming. Why didn't the Fox press her more about Sam's whereabouts? And if the Fox knew he was being set up, why go through with the facade? Ant's desk phone came to life as the questions swelled inside my head.

"Lieutenant Ant, here," barking into the phone. "What?" His voice changed within seconds of talking to whoever was on the other end. "When? Alright, I'll be right over."

After dropping the phone back down into its cradle, he stared long and hard at the surface of his desk as though he'd lost something. And he didn't look happy. His expression had shifted from anger to concern. He turned his attention back to us and said, "Miguel's escaped."

24

THE BOEING 737 was twenty minutes late. Zero felt relief when it finally touched down. Besides rain, flying was his second pet peeve. Zero had no problem killing in cold blood or even being shot to death in a shootout—if it came to that. But flying? Forget it. He didn't like that his life was in the hands of someone he'd never met and that the whole thing was surreal—seventy-one tons of steel moving through space.

At least, in a face-off with the cops, he could go down in glory and with guns blazing. What was also frustrating was that when he flew, he had to take medication to calm his nerves, causing him not to completely control his faculties.

Once through customs and security, he retrieved his one piece of luggage and headed directly to the car rental booth. He booked a nondescript, white Toyota Corolla, two-door, wanting to blend into traffic and not bring any undue attention to himself. He then drove to a small motel off the highway on Motor City's outskirts. After checking in under the pseudonym of Mr. Marquis, he unpacked his only piece of luggage.

It contained several recently pressed bleach-white cotton shirts, a pair of tan trousers—its seams also ironed to perfection, a pair of black jeans, underwear, and socks. He deposited these items into the wood-grained dresser behind him. A small leather bag that held his toiletry, he moved to the bathroom.

The only item remaining was his hunter's knife, shielded in a leather sheath. He pulled it out to give it a quick once over. It had a six-inch clip-point steel blade with a serrated edge. Placing it in his open palm, he admired its weight and balance. The knife had a traditional black phenolic handle with palm swells allowing for a comfortable grip. The aluminum pommel/guard added to its classic style, beauty, and balance. Giving the knife a few more moments of admiration, he placed it back into its leather sheath, then snapped close the fastener to keep the blade secure. He partially undid his pant belt and looped it through the sheath's integrated belt loop, positioning it near his back.

A smirk crossed Zero's face. He was thinking how ironic it was that one could legally own and carry such an item providing your intent was not for criminal purposes. But how would someone know until they acted on that impulse? He put on his black suit coat and took one last look around the room. Then exited.

25

I WAS AT A DEAD END—out of leads and with no idea what to do next. The Feds were tight-lipped about what happened with Miguel's escape. They'd only say that while transporting the prisoner to a maximum-security dark site, unknown perps ambushed the transport, and the prisoner escaped.

That night I polished off a half bottle of bourbon and inhaled a couple of packs of smokes. Finally, at around two in the morning, I dropped off into a peaceful slumber. After a quick shower and shave the following day, I headed over to Gracie's Diner, pondering my next move.

"Why the glum face, James?" Gracie asked but didn't wait for an answer. "It can mean only one thing. You're on a tough case, and you're stumped."

"You know me all too well, Gracie," offering a strained smile.

"Can't it be worse than this virus that's going around?"

"What virus—" I went to say but cut myself short, recalling the broadcast I had seen the other day at Pat's. "Oh, that one. What's the status on it?"

"Well, they're saying they found traces of it right here in Motor City."

"That can't be good."

"You're telling me. Business is already down by twenty percent. People are getting scared to go out."

"But what I heard, it's not that deadly."

"Well, the doctors have been changing their tune. Now they're not so sure. But then again, people fear what they don't know or understand."

"Gracie, you're so much wiser than your years."

"You know, your compliments won't get you a free breakfast," she said, smiling.

"Would never think of it. You're already practically giving them away at these prices."

"Well, enjoy it while you can. I can only do that because of the volume of customers that move through here. If that level drops further, I'll have to jack up the prices."

"That'd be a real shame."

"Speaking of shame, Anne keeps asking about you. It seems you two hit it off, but you always have a cockamamie excuse on why you can't see her."

"They're not excuses. I'm a busy man," I said. "I mean, sure, I like her, and we had a great time, but…."

Gracie gave me a long motherly look, then said, "You know, James, you're not getting any younger, and there comes a time in one's life to commit to someone. To find love. Or they end up alone with no one to care for them."

"Well, I'll take that under consideration, o-wise-one, but can we get down to the actual business at hand—my breakfast."

"As you wish. The customer is always right."

I had only gotten through one egg, two strips of bacon and a half dozen home fries before Sangria showed up.

"Ant was right." Sangria bellowed out upon seeing me.

"Oh, why's that," I said, looking up.

"He said that you head here whenever you're stumped on a case."

"It's time to shake up my routine. The entire world seems privy to my habits. So, what brings you here? It can't just be to prove Ant's hypothesis."

"Well, the way you ran out of Ant's office the other day, we didn't have time to discuss any ideas. And what was that thing with Piña all about?"

"Let's just say it was getting a bit too claustrophobic."

"You're having second thoughts about her?"

"Why do you say that?"

"I saw how you reacted when she came over to you. And then you kept avoiding her glances."

"I'd say it was the other way around?"

"It's funny, isn't it?

"What's that?"

"No matter how old we get, we still fall for the same old mating rituals."

"I've no idea what you're talking about. Either sit down and order something, or we can meet later to discuss your cryptic ideas. My breakfast is getting cold."

Sangria opted for the former, ordering breakfast and a cup of black coffee. We did small talk until Gracie brought Sangria his chow and left; I then asked, "So, what's on your mind?"

"Well, there's nothing new to report on Miguel's escape. When I talked to Ant earlier this morning, he said the Feds are still mum of the situation. So, he's trying to pull favors to see if he can't loosen a few tongues."

"I wouldn't hold my breath. What else?"

"I was in touch with my head office."

"And?" I asked, forcing me to pry the information from him.

"An associate of Miguel's, who goes by the name of Zero, flew out of Buenos Aires last night. And he's heading our way."

"That's interesting. What's with the name?"

"No one knows. But one thing's for sure."

"Oh. What's that?"

"He's a cold-blooded assassin. And Miguel and Zero have a history dating back to the Dirty Wars."

"Funny how it always comes back to the wars. I've been thinking about how a certain thread in time never leaves us. How it always comes back to haunt us."

"Heady stuff first thing in the morning, James."

"Can't help it. I get like this when things feel like they're spinning out of control."

"What's this thread you're talking about?" Sangria asked, concerned.

"You've heard about the virus that's been going around."

"Yeah, I heard something about it in the news."

"I guess you didn't hear the part about it originating in Antwerp." I let this latest piece of information sink in for a beat.

"Do you think there's something to it?"

"Not sure, but let's sum up what do we know so far? This whole thing started with Stonewall hiring me to find a missing orangutan. Then a diamond and a dead body later, Miguel offs Stonewall and frames me for it. Later he meets with some Mafioso to exchange the gems for something, but we have no idea what or why."

"Then he lets himself get caught only to escape," Sangria added.

"And now you tell me an associate of Miguel, a cold-blooded killer, is in town. So, what's it all boils down to?"

"No idea."

"Exactly. We got zilch. Miguel's running circles around us. "

"Oh, I forgot to mention one other thing. They found Don Carmella's godson dead in Buenos Aires. Stabbed to death in a cemetery."

"It figures. It couldn't be as simple hit on a deserted back street."

"And it fits Zero's MO."

"Great. All we need is two homicidal maniacs on the loose in Motor City. My head's starting to ache."

"Based on your city's homicide rates, two more won't make that much difference."

"Not in the short run, but something tells me that we're heading for a perfect storm with these two on the loose. And we'd better find them before the entire city crumbles around us.

26

PIÑA WASN'T SURE why James reacted the way he did. Perhaps he didn't want his emotions displayed in front of the others. This was one of the most distressing and dysfunctional attributes with all the men she'd dated. But that's where the similarities ended. She knew deep down; James was a troubled and sensitive soul. She couldn't imagine what he'd experienced in his profession—the violence, depravity, and misery of his work.

Up to a point, that is. She'd seen how inhumanely humans treated other species—corralling animals into industrialized slaughterhouses or triggering the extinction of hundreds of species through global warming and deforestation. Soon our species' turn will come. The spread of the latest virus was a sign.

She sensed James suspected her of something. And he wouldn't be too far off from the truth. A lawyer representing a wealthy, anonymous benefactor approached her five months earlier. He had a proposition that she found hard to refuse.

The lawyer explained that the benefactor had contacts with the Basel Zoo and that the zoo was having financial difficulties. They also sought a facility to take one of their baby orangutans.

So, they arranged to transfer the orangutan to the Chicago Zoo in exchange for financial help from the benefactor. Piña had asked why her zoo. The lawyer explained that the benefactor had heard remarkable things about her work and wanted to contribute further to her research.

What a fool she'd been. She now realized that the benefactor was likely Miguel. He had used her to smuggle the gems in. Now it was too late. If she told anyone, she'd be implicated as one of his co-conspirators—and lose James in the process.

27

MIGUEL HAD PLANNED his escape to the very last detail. Thanks to an inside source, he knew the intimate details of his transfer beforehand—the route the Feds would take and their use of three identical vehicles, usually black Ford SUVs—two acting as decoys and one holding the prisoner for transport to a secure facility. They'd also use air support to survey any abnormalities. The vehicles would veer off in separate directions at the first sign of trouble.

So, Miguel devised a plan accordingly. His men ambushed the caravan as it passed under the i75 overpass at Davison Freeway, plunging a vehicle into oncoming traffic, causing multiple casualties and chaos. His men then swooped in, executing his escape without a hitch.

Miguel couldn't help but smile, recalling Cartwright's reaction to the Feds snatching his prize from right under his nose. Though Cartwright had acted with surprise and indignation, Miguel figured the PI knew something was amiss by the looks and questions he was getting.

But in the end, Cartwright couldn't put the pieces together. This gave Miguel the most incredible joy—this game of cat and mouse. It's why he allowed himself to be captured. He knew that news of the orangutan's capture was fake. If Cartwright had found the gems, he wouldn't have taken the chance of leaking the fact, especially with his beloved Piña under his control. Miguel had played along to see if he could get away with it. But he also wanted to get a closer look and gauge Cartwright before making his final decision.

He had to admit that Cartwright's stern Americana look attracted him—those rugged facial features, his busted-up, crooked nose, full lips, and deep dark penetrating brown eyes. And then there was that black overcoat of his that looked like moths had been feasting on it for years. And that damn fedora he wore made him look like something from a Humphrey Bogart movie. Miguel would miss him when this was all over.

He picked up his cell phone and dialed a number, waiting for the predetermined ten rings before a female voice answered, "I've been expecting your call."

"Is it arranged?" Miguel asked the woman on the other end.

"We can't find him."

"What do you mean you can't find him?" Miguel demanded, exasperated.

"He's disappeared. The last time we spotted him, he was boarding a plane at Ministro Pistarini International Airport."

"Where to?"

The woman on the other end of the line paused momentarily, not wanting to be the bearer of bad news. Finally, she said, "he's on his way to you. To Motor City."

"Jesus Christ! What do I pay you for?" Miguel shouted at the women on the other end and hung up. That's all he needed—to be fighting a war on two fronts.

But he couldn't worry about that now. His priority was to rid himself of that pesky PI. He knew Cartwright would never give up. He had an unhealthy sense of curiosity akin to a death wish. Miguel needed a more permanent solution to his problem.

He made another call.

THE LONG SLEEP

28

I SLOWLY ROUSED myself from the nightmare. The slamming of fists at my front door demanded my attention. My first thought was that a thunderstorm of biblical proportions had descended on Motor City.

The nightmare had rattled me.

In it, I found myself navigating an array of tunnels deep beneath the earth's surface. And no matter which passageway I took, I'd end up back in the same place—within a circular enclosure filled with indecipherable glyphs. I had no idea what the glyphs meant—if they were Egyptian, Sumerian or had been left there by little gray aliens visiting the planet centuries earlier.

After a dozen attempts to decipher the glyphs, fatigue set in, and I sat myself down within the enclosure's center. Then I heard footsteps— faint at first but increasing in volume. Someone or thing was making its way through the tunnels. I couldn't be sure if these recent developments were actual or illusions and had no idea how long I'd been down here. It felt like forever.

Finally, a thin, weary-looking man appeared through one of the passageways. He looked to be in his late forties. His skin was a deathly pale white. His shaved head had tattoo markings all over it. His crystalline cold-blue eyes jumped out—a bright madness seeping through. He was wearing what looked to be a white medical gown and was clutching an oversized scalpel in his right hand. Slivers of candlelight danced off the blade's silver-plated surface as he approached.

"Who are you? What do you want?" I shouted out, terrified, hoping to halt his progress.

"It's time," replied the whitewashed stranger.

"For what?"

"For the end times. You are to be my first sacrifice."

"What the hell are you—"

"Cartwright! Cartwright! Are you in there?" A voice shouted, joining the incessant hammering at my front door. I reluctantly got up and threw on my pants and shirt, exiting the bedroom with remnants of the dream lingering in my head. Opening the door, I confronted Lieutenant Ant and two uniform cops standing behind him.

"What the hell, Ant—"

"You're under arrest, Cartwright. For the murder of Miss Veronica Stonewall," he stated in his official cop voice.

"Come off it, Ant, you know Miguel framed me. I told you the how and by who."

"I know, Cartwright. But I still need to bring you in. Her body washed up along the river last night. We also have a warrant to search your house and office."

"And here I thought we were friends. That I could trust you."

"I am, and you can. You know that. That's why I came in person. To ensure no trigger-happy cop cuts you down and that the search is by the book."

"Next, you'll tell me I'll get a fair trial."

"It won't come to that," Ant said unconvincingly.

"And how do you know that? This guy's been two steps ahead of us so far. Has something changed?"

"You gotta trust the system."

"Oh, that speech again. You know, one day, you'll wake up and realize that there's no such thing. It's a jungle out there, as they say. And only the fittest and shrewdest of the species survive to fight another day."

"You don't believe that—"

"Get down!" I shouted, diving for Ant—the momentum carrying us both onto the front lawn. A hail of bullets from the Uzis that two bikers had aimed at us ignited the morning air. The two uniform cops had no idea what hit them. I pulled Ant's service revolver from his shoulder holster, having left the Colt inside, and let off several rounds, one connecting with one biker's left shoulder. He skidded out of control, tumbling onto the ground. His partner raced to his aid. The fallen biker, now on his feet, jumped onto the back of his partner's bike. They fired off one last desperate round before disappearing down the street.

Figuring the coast was clear, Ant and I got up. I couldn't help firing off a barb of my own at Ant. "What was that you were saying about a fair system?"

Ant said nothing. He hurried toward the two downed officers to check for a pulse. I could have saved him the trouble. Even from where I was standing, their fate was a foregone conclusion.

Returning, he said, "Jesus, Cartwright. What a mess. This changes everything. You don't mess with my boys and walk away from it. What a waste. And for what?"

"It's obvious. I'm getting under Miguel's skin. Or why send his boys."

"But he already had me on that murder rap."

"I guess he figures that wouldn't hold. Perhaps he was also gunning for me this time," Ant speculated.

"Could be. But this tells me that something big is about to happen. Miguel wants to make sure that I or anyone else that can interfere with his plan is out of the way."

"Yeah. But what plan?"

"That's the twenty-million-dollar question. It all started with that diamond heist. And we're still no closer to knowing why or what he intends to do with the sale of those gems."

"Whatever it is, it's worth killing for."

"So, now what, Ant? Still taking me in?" I said, extending my arms in a gesture to cuff them. We could hear the distant screech of the police sirens fast approaching.

Giving me a long, reflective stare, he finally said, "I'll tell them I knocked, but before anyone answered, these goons attacked us. Maybe you were home. Maybe you weren't. So, I'd suggest you get the hell out of here before someone confirms the opposite."

"Why the change of heart, Lieutenant?"

"Let's just say I owe you one. I wouldn't be here if it weren't for your quick actions. Besides, we both know you didn't murder Stonewall. I'll cover as long as I can. But promise me, you'll get this son-of-a-bitch."

"You can bet on it," I said, reassuring him.

"And remember, there's still a warrant out for your arrest. You'll need to keep a low profile. You can't contact me at the 3rd. I'll get a burner phone to you through Elvis. We can keep in touch that way."

"Burner phone?"

"I keep forgetting you're from another century. Don't worry. Elvis can explain. But you gotta move," he said, followed by a weak smile.

The sirens were increasing in volume. They'd be here any minute. Ant turned his attention back to the fallen officers. I followed suit, both of us offering a moment of silence to the men. Then, without another word, I ran inside to retrieve my Colt, and out the backdoor, down the alley and back onto the street where my caddy was parked—got in and gunned it out of there. In the rear-view mirror, I glimpsed the cruisers, with their red and blue beacons screaming—braking hard in front of my place. I had gotten out just in time.

29

THE ONLY OTHER TIME I'd seen Ant in such a state was when he lost his teenage son in a shootout between local gangs. He tracked them down, including the one who pulled the trigger. The perp was only fifteen. His son was only seventeen. So, what could he do?

Ant had strong morals but also limits—cop or no cop. Lucky for the banger, morals won out that day. With the senseless killing of the two cops, Ant had reached a breaking point. Fuck morals and his badge. He'd do whatever it took to bring Fox down, even if it meant destroying his career.

Ant and I agreed on something for once. This was no time to burrow in like some pocket gopher. It was time for action, and I figured Piña was an excellent place to start. I had two reasons for this. One was to clear up what happened the other day in Ant's office. The other had to do with my strong suspicions that she was keeping something from me, something to do with Miguel. As far as I knew, she was still staying at Baymont Hotel on East Jefferson. A pleasant enough place and a few blocks down from the Motown Museum, where Berry Gordy, Jr. had lived and recorded some of the most extraordinary acts for Motown Records.

A scrawny young man with beet-red hair stood behind the hotel counter. He greeted me with a suspect smile. I asked if a Piña Cornell was registered there. He punched in a few keystrokes, then looked up from the monitor and asked why. I told him I wanted to speak with her, wanting to add it was none of his business. Begrudgingly, he announced my presence to her via the hotel phone, then told me to go up. She was staying in room 222.

I took the stairs to the second floor, but as was always the case, I turned the wrong way. There was some conspiracy with hotels and their hallways. They set them up like mazes, forcing unsuspecting visitors to get lost the first time. And once you found the door, you were so relieved and excited, as though you'd won the jackpot. Piña answered on the first knock.

"James?" she said more a question than a statement.

"Hello Piña, I hope I'm not disturbing you?" I said, sounding like a school kid selling cookies. What was it with me? I was constantly reverting to my childhood whenever I saw her.

"No. It's fine. I was just packing. Getting ready to go back."

"I see. And you weren't going to tell me? To let me know?"

"I thought you made your intent very clear at the Lieutenant's office the other day."

"Yeah. About that. That's one reason I'm here. I want to explain."

"What's there to explain?"

"Well, I… I just wanted it to appear professional, you know, about our relationship in front of Ant and Sangria."

"I didn't even know we had a relationship. All we did was share some fish 'n' chips together one night."

"I don't just share fish' n' chips with anyone, you know," I offered, trying to get a smile. It worked.

"I see. So, where does that leave us?"

I had no answer. I didn't expect such a direct question. But I guess the signs were there about how we felt for each other. I was never good at those sorts of things. Especially expressing my feelings. They could get me killed. And when it came to reading the subtle signs of creeps and murderers, that was another story. But forget it when it came to women. I seemed to lose all sense of rhyme or reason. My judgement became clouded.

"To be honest, I'm not sure and haven't given it much thought," I finally answered.

"Oh."

"What I mean is that I like you. I like you a lot, but with everything that's been happening, well—"

"It's OK, James, I understand." But before I knew what was happening, she planted a short but passionate kiss across my lips, then pulled back, searching my face for any signs of protest. We flung ourselves onto the bed, losing ourselves in the moment, overwhelmed by our passion and lust. We spent the next few hours lost in our entanglement. When we finally came up for air, we just lay there in silence for a good half hour, enjoying the warmth of each other's bodies. Piña was the first to break the silence.

"There's something I have to tell you, James."

"What's that?" I asked, turning on my side to face her. She kept staring up at the ceiling.

"A few months back, this lawyer came to see me."

"About what?" I asked, curious.

"You're not going to like what I'm about to say. That's why I waited so long."

"Piña, what is it?" I asked, concerned. "You know you can trust me."

"Well, a few months back, this lawyer came to see me and told me he could arrange for the Chicago Zoo to get a baby orangutan."

"Ombak?"

"Yes."

"And?"

Tears started leaking from the corner of her eyes. She reached up to wipe them away. But with little luck. I grabbed some tissues from the night table and handed them to her. The pushed on.

"I'm sorry, Piña, but you must tell me everything."

"The lawyer said that he represented a wealthy benefactor who could arrange the whole thing because the Basel Zoo was having financial difficulties."

"The Fox?" I guessed.

"I didn't know that then. I swear it, James."

I got up, taking my anger out on my pants, jamming them up one leg, then the other, and almost toppling over a few times. Then without looking at Piña, I paced the room, trying to understand the implications of what she had just told me. What she'd done wasn't necessarily illegal. It was just plain dumb—not verifying who the lawyer was and who he was representing. And there was probably enough circumstantial evidence to put her in a heap of trouble. She'd probably lose her job and could be charged as an accessory if Ant wanted to be an asshole.

"Don't be so hard on yourself," I finally said. "We were both had. This guy plays a mean con. He suckered me with Miss Stonewall."

And that's when the idea hit me. "By any chance, did you get the lawyer's name?" I asked, having stopped pacing.

"He gave me his card, if that's what you're asking?"

"Do you have it with you?"

"No. It's back in my office."

"Probably not," I countered. "Miguel or one of his goons would have retrieved it by now. Can you remember the lawyer's name or the firm he worked for?"

"Why, what good would it do? His name was surely not real."

"Not necessarily. In case you had him checked out, Fox probably hired a legitimate law firm."

"That makes sense. Now, let's see. It was something like Mike Spin, Trine, no. No. Wait a minute. Flynn. It was Michael Flynn. That's it. And his last name was part of the firm's name, which I recall had two other names attached."

"That's a good start."

"What do you have in mind?"

"It may be our Hail Mary to track Miguel down. All the other leads have dried up. Plus, he tried to have me killed today."

"What?" Piña shouted, jumping out of the bed and embracing to me. "Why didn't you tell me this when you came in?"

"Didn't want to get you all crazy, the way you're acting now."

But suddenly, realizing she was only wearing her birthday suit, she offered a mischievous and seductive smile. She started caressing me across my spine, followed by quick pecks with her lips along my neck and shoulders. The lower she went, the further I fell headlong into oblivion.

30

ANT VISITED the families of the fallen officers to notify them of what had happened. One officer was recently married and had a three-year-old daughter. The other was single but had close ties to his extended family. This was always the most challenging part of his job. There was no simple way to tell the families what had happened. He could only offer the standard pitch that they were heroes and died in the line of duty. But to be gunned down the way they had been was something else.

One could argue it was part of the job. But Ant never bought into that bull for a minute. No cop ever signed up to get themselves killed in the line of duty unless they had some screw loose—and there had been a few. There were those with racial or sadistic tendencies who gave the Force a lousy name. But mostly, his men were idealists, believing in the code to serve and protect. And Cartwright had been one of those.

Ant thought back to when he first met Cartwright. He was still green behind the ears, having just gotten his detective's shield and believing he could change the world. He was drinking at a local cop bar when Cartwright approached him, proclaiming he'd solved a case.

Cartwright's naivety and enthusiasm amused Ant. This rookie thought he had single-handedly solved a case that a task force of some twenty seasoned officers couldn't do.

But Cartwright's analysis of the case impressed him. He'd figured out who the unsub was and where he'd strike next. The problem was he'd obtained the information without following proper procedures. And it was all circumstantial. Ant couldn't go to the higher-ups with what he had brought him or get proper warrants. And told him so.

Cartwright went into a rant, claiming how justice was blind. How all this impartiality, objectivity, and bloated bureaucracy stifled his abilities. How the system would never stop the violence riddling the streets of Motor City.

"We're merely trash collectors, showing up after the fact to dispose of the victims," he claimed angrily and frustrated. Ant knew then and there that Cartwright wouldn't last long on the Force. He didn't have that sense of brotherhood and comradery. He was a lone wolf.

Even though Cartwright had a good point, Ant couldn't tell him that. Not then. So, he gave him his template speech about justice and how we couldn't go around being judge, jury and executioner. And how one couldn't force the facts to fit the crime. One had to have patience and believe in due process.

Ant took a final hard look at the two-burner phones he bought on the way to the office. He knew that there was no turning back once he did what he was about to do.

Fuck it, he said out loud to himself, slipping one phone into his inside suit coat pocket, and headed for his car in the 3rd precinct parking lot. He had an appointment to keep with Elvis.

31

IT TOOK ZERO less than an hour to track down Fox's lair but two to get there due to the traffic. He never understood America's love affair with cars and their masochistic need to sit for hours on end in traffic jams. Miguel's hideout was in Grosse Pointe, about a twenty-five-minute ride outside Motor City. Leave it to Miguel to choose such an affluent area. Such a hypocrite, Zero thought to himself.

Miguel's house was one of the largest along the strip, measuring some ten-thousand square feet and built in the New-Georgian manner. Also, the Lakeview yacht club was a mile away. Zero figured Miguel probably had a boat docked there in case of a quick getaway.

Taking out a set of binoculars, he started surveying the premises. He made out at least five men guarding the front and most likely a few stationed in the back for good measure. A few of the men he recognized from his meetings with Miguel. And they were not to be trifled with. He knew their strengths but also their limitations. Since Zero detested firearms, he'd have to get up close to neutralize them, but he'd have to wait till nightfall.

So, he made himself comfortable behind the dense foliage that grew along the incline several hundred yards from the place. He pulled a brown paper bag from the gray canvas bag. He had prepared some sandwiches made of lettuce, sliced tomatoes and a heaping dose of salt. He was a vegetarian by choice. He abhorred how animals were raised for slaughter. He then pulled out a thermos filled with his favorite drink called Yerba-mate—a caffeinated tea first cultivated by the Indigenous Guaraní in southern Brazil. Now he was all set. He sat back and waited for the night to fall.

32

DR. EMANUEL DEGAS was pleased with the progress his virus had made. The World Health Organization and other world scientists still hadn't figured out its true purpose. They only understood how it spread—through contaminated surfaces and aerosol transmission. Symptoms such as high fever, sore throat, and a cough appeared anywhere from a week or two after infection, making it difficult to control the transmission rate. Some of those infected were asymptomatic, while others showed minor symptoms which faded after a few days with no apparent damage. But there were exceptions. A few poor souls—five percent of those infected- died from complications.

The pandemic also caused panic selling in the international money markets. There was talk of shutting down schools, government agencies, and large chain outlets to slow its spread. Miguel had been right. His plan was playing out as he predicted. And Emanuel would finally have revenge for his son's death.

After leaving Piña, I went looking for Elvis. This time, I found him on my first try at his usual haunt on Bagley and 24th, pawning knockoffs.

Since a BOLO was out for my arrest, I had walked ten blocks from Piña's hotel.

"Well, well, well," he said, as he caught sight of me, "you've finally taken my advice about getting some exercise."

"When have I ever taken your advice on life choices seriously?"

"You've got a point there. But what happened to your caddy?"

"Long story short, I'm on the lam. I'm suspected of killing that insurance dame."

"The one you told me about. The one Fox framed you for."

"Yep. That's the one."

"Damn, James, you are one to get yourself into a pickle."

"Any chance our favorite lieutenant dropped by?"

"As a matter of fact, he did. He left me a burner phone for you. I asked him what was happening, but he wasn't in any mood to talk. I've never seen him like that. Then I heard about the two cops shot dead. Got me thinking."

"Fox was gunning for me and missed. The two cops weren't so lucky."

"I should start calling you the Cat. But that wouldn't work. Since I've known you, you should've met your maker a dozen times over."

"Thanks for that, Elvis. Nothing like having someone clock my death march."

"Just saying, that's all. But I'll be damned if something happens to you on my watch."

"Good to know. About that burner phone."

"Yeah, it's safely stashed away at my place. We might as well head over now. Nothing's happening here. Business has been at a standstill ever since that virus hit. Everyone's running scared. Not good for business."

"Well, I guess if someone has to choose between a Gucci and their health, the choice seems clear."

"Funny guy. Wait till your clients dry up."

"Hardly doubtful. Virus or no virus, murder ain't going to stop. It's in our nature. If anything, it's about to go up."

33

I CALLED ANT on the burner phone but got no reply. I then called Sangria. He answered on the second ring.

"Sangria, here."

"Sangria, it's me, Cartwright."

"James. What the hell? Where are you? The whole goddamn police force is looking for you."

"I'll explain later. Meet me in an hour at the Anthology Café over on Division St," I said, then hung up.

I had just caught sight of a patrol car heading my way. I wasn't sure if I'd been spotted, but I wasn't about to test fate. I ducked into an alleyway several feet away. But before I realized it, the laneway dead-ended about a hundred feet behind me. The cruiser had stopped, and two uniforms got out.

One of the cops yelled over, "Hey you."

I tried to think fast, but nothing came. That's when I heard the door open behind me. The butcher from the shop that fronted the street was just exiting, hauling several trash bags to the dumpster. Streaks of dried red blood smeared his once pristine white uniform. I ran toward him.

As I did, I heard one of the cops repeat their warning, "Hey, stop where you are!" I assumed he had also drawn his gun.

The butcher dropped the bags, startled by the commotion, causing one to split open. Rotting flesh and dark-purple-red-stained bones splattered to the ground, adding further to the collection of blood on his shoes and uniform. As I reached him, he made no move to stop me but raised his hands in surrender, stepping aside to let me pass.

I was betting on the two cops making a rookie mistake. And they did. They ran after me instead of splitting up, having one cover the front door. I couldn't blame them. In their line of work, they were always making split-second decisions—sometimes the right one, but fortunately for me, the wrong one today.

Once inside the shop, a few customers screamed, startled by my sudden appearance, including a middle-aged brunette who I figured to be the butcher's wife—also adorning a blood-stained apron. I offered a stupid grin, pulled out my PI ID, and said, "City inspector. Just go back to what you were doing."

But no one moved as they watched me vault over the counter and push through the front door like a jack-in-the-box. I made directly for the cop's curser, figuring that today they'd double their odds in the fuck-up department.

I was right. They left the car running. I jumped into the driver's seat and peeled out. I spotted the two cops as they exited the front, looking like they'd just gotten star roles in a Buster Keaton movie. I dumped the cruiser, about eight blocks from the café where I was meeting Sangria and walked the rest. The way things were going, Elvis's suggestion of getting more exercise was becoming a reality.

Sangria was already waiting for me by the time I got there. He had ordered a double espresso. I did likewise since the café offered nothing more substantial.

"James, you're taking quite a risk meeting out in the open like this."

"What am I supposed to do, hideout in some abandoned warehouse or back alleys like a wounded animal?" I said, smiling and thinking about my recent encounter with the cops, the butcher, and his wife.

"I would."

"And how would I go about clearing my name?"

"Leave it to me and Ant. We'll do what it takes."

"Ant's a good man, but he's bound by duty. And you're a foreigner and don't have access to dig deep enough. But I need your help for something else."

"What? Name it."

"We may have caught a break. I tracked down a lawyer who did work for Miguel."

"How'd you do that?"

"A confidential informant," I said. He knew I was lying but didn't push the issue. "Before calling you, I had Elvis check on this guy. The lawyer is Michael Flynn of Flynn, Massy, and Martin over on Hillside."

"And what do you want me to do, exactly?" His expression told me he didn't like where this was going.

"I need you to visit him. Rattle his cage. Obviously, I can't. I'm on Motor City's top ten hit list. Just mention that you're with Interpol, which you are, and that he's under investigation for bank fraud."

"But we don't do bank fraud."

"You do when it's tied to international money laundering. And that one of his clients is a known felon."

"He's just going to plead the fifth and demand to see a lawyer?" Sangria said, deflecting. It was obvious his heart wasn't into my idea.

"Did I mention his firm has an office in Buenos Aires?"

"No kidding?"

"I had Elvis hack his financial transactions and travel itinerary. It looks like he's been getting major kickbacks from someone out of Miguel's hometown. Plus, he's traveled there a half dozen times this year."

"You've done your homework."

"Now it's your turn to grade it and see if it gets top marks."

"What are you going to do while I bait the hook?"

"Try to figure out where the hell that missing orangutan has gotten to?"

"Oh yeah. I forgot about her. I guess she's still on the loose?"

"As far as I know. And I still think if I can find her, it'd break the case wide open."

"How so?"

"If I knew that, I wouldn't have to find her. It's a bit of a Catch-22."

"I see. Well, I better get moving on this lawyer. How do I get a hold of you?"

"Call me at this number," I said, pulling out my burner. "But first, I need to shower and have a quick nap. Haven't slept in two days."

"Are you crazy? They'll have your place staked out."

"Not likely. But I'll have Ant take care of it if that's the case. As you said, I've got friends."

Sangria offered to drive me to the office, but I declined. I didn't want to jeopardize his career if we got pulled over. Besides, I was enjoying my walks. It had a way of clearing the head, allowing me to focus on what was important. Which I desperately needed to do.

The case had busted into a dozen incomprehensible puzzles, with no idea how to piece it back together.

34

I HAD ANOTHER DREAM. I was once again in the cavern deep beneath the earth's surface. The passages were still there, but there was no sign of the pale stranger. The alien-like glyphs were now glowing, pulsating a deep cadmium yellow. The more I stared at them, the more they shifted—their movements synced to some inaudible music or rhythm. I counted twenty-four the last time but realized that only twenty remained.

Puzzled, I surveyed my surroundings, spotting the four missing glyphs. They were moving out from each of the four passages. One from the south. Another from the north and the last two from the east and west. But what made the situation even more bizarre was how they were increasing in size. Having surrounded me and a mere two feet away, they mutated into orangutans. And they didn't seem happy.

But before I could figure out why, I woke up. The burner phone that Ant had given me was demanding my attention.

"Yeah, Cartwright here," I shouted into it.

"It's me, Sangria," the voice on the other end said, almost inaudible.

"Speak up, Sangria. I can hardly hear you."

"I can't. Meet me at Ninth and Cumberland as soon as you can. It's an abandoned warehouse. I think I've—"

"What? I didn't hear that last part." But got no answer. The phone had gone dead.

As I navigated to the location Sangria had given me, the streets held a deathly silence—one I had never felt before. Unlike the suburbs and gated communities surrounding it, Motor City was always full of life at any hour of the day. People were usually out for a stroll, bar hopping to various nightclubs, or out killing each other. There was always something going on. But this damn virus had stopped the city in its track. Something not even the National Guard could do during the '67 riots.

It took a good twenty minutes to walk to Sangria's location. But once I got there, I saw no sign of Sangria. The place looked as dead as the streets I had encountered earlier. The fire-red paint that once adorned the place had cracked and peeled over the years. One could still make out the company's faded name and a logo that read Darnell Chemicals. I wondered what chemicals they had produced as I moved cautiously to the central double glass front doors.

Sneaking a peek inside, a small reception area stared back at me, void of any furniture or fixtures that may have once littered its space. I now decided to make my way to the back of the building. Again, no sign of Sangria. I climbed the stairs leading up to a loading dock.

The padlock that once secured the sizeable overhead door had been cracked open. I took a deep breath and pulled the door up. It gave way with some effort, squeaking in protest to my attempt. I stood to the side and listened. Nothing.

I moved in, using the Colt in my outstretched arm as a guide. It took a minute to adjust to the interior darkness. I was breathing hard from the adrenaline rushing through my veins. But met no resistance.

There was only one solitary figure sharing the space with me. It was Sangria. He was hanging eight feet above the ground—a noose wrapped around his neck.

I called Ant to let him know what happened, then skipped out before the troops arrived. There'd be time to mourn my friend, but now wasn't it.

END OF DAYS

35

BY THE TIME I returned to the office, the day was breaking. I swept the area, ensuring none of Motor City's finest were around, and entered through the back entrance. Once safely inside my office, the answering machine alerted me that I had new messages.

I gave them a quick listen, but only one caught my attention. An anonymous caller claimed to know where I could find the Fox. It was an address over in Grosse Pointe. I wasn't sure what to make of it or who the caller was. Most likely a trap. But I had no choice. I had to follow up.

Along the way, I got my thermos filled with strong black coffee from a local cafe to keep my pint of bourbon company. One was to keep me awake, the other to keep me warm in case I had to stake out the place all night. The days had been getting cooler as fall neared.

Also, before leaving the office, I called Ant to check for any progress on Sangria's killer. Ant said he put a BOLO out on Flynn, the lawyer, but so far, no luck. He had either flown the coop or was swimming with the walleyes at the bottom of the Detroit River.

But both Ant and I agreed that the Fox was behind this. Who else would have the motive to see Sangria dead, apart from the lawyer? And from what Elvis had told me, Flynn didn't strike me as the cold-blooded killer type.

Ant said that Sangria had contacted the lawyer, as I suggested. The secretary verified this. Sangria met with Flynn that afternoon. Then Flynn canceled all his appointments for the rest of the day, leaving twenty minutes later. He had been in a hurry. From that point forward, the lawyer's and Sangria's movements were unknown, that is, until I found Sangria at the abandoned warehouse.

Besides losing my last solid lead, I also lost a good partner. Even a friend. Though I'd only known him for three short days, I was beginning to see him as a kindred spirit. I felt anger rising in my throat. I pushed it back. I had reached my destination.

I found a spot in a small, wooded enclave a thousand feet from the house to set up and survey the situation. The place had a six-foot iron-wrought fence that ran along its perimeter. I spotted three men in black suits—the type Fox's goons were accustomed to wearing, patrolling the grounds. I didn't recognize any of their ugly mugs, but most likely, they were heavily armed.

So, for the moment, all I could was wait and see if an opportunity arose. I pulled out the thermos of coffee I had brought and went to pour some.

That's when I felt a sharp pin prick in my lower back, followed by a determined voice, "Easy does it, my friend." I recognized it right off. It was the voice from the machine.

I knew better than to turn around. I assumed whoever this guy was wouldn't hesitate to use the blade.

"What do you want?"

"The same thing you do," he volleyed.

"What would that be?"

"To take down a mutual enemy."

"Oh yeah. And who's that?"

"Quit playing games, Cartwright."

"I see you know who I am. But I'm clueless about your identity," I countered, even though I had a strong hunch he was the assassin Sangria had told me about. "Why not enlighten me?"

"That's not important. What's imperative is accomplishing our mutual goal."

"And this is the way you ask for help?"

"Not usually. Whenever I pull my blade, someone usually dies. Consider yourself the exception." He had a strong accent like Sangria— of Italian descent.

"Understood, but why the charade?"

"Better this way. I'd prefer that you can't identify me once our business ends. Then there'll be no need for this," pushing the knife's point further toward my kidney. I was sure he had drawn blood.

"So, what do you want?" I asked, in what I hoped was a steady voice, trying to ignore the pain.

"Miguel isn't here. I've been staking the place out for the past two days. But I persuaded one of his goons to offer up a bit of vital information."

"Oh, yeah. What's that?"

"Miguel's on his way to Montreal."

"Canada?"

"Where else?" he replied, with a hint of sarcasm.

"But why?" I asked more to myself. I was trying to get my head around this infuriating puzzle that kept adding pieces to itself without rhyme or reason.

"That's what I need you to find out."

"Why me? Why not go yourself?"

"It was tough enough, just getting here. I don't have the resources to get myself into Canada. Besides, someone needs to watch this place."

"Trouble is, I only accept clients during normal business hours."

"I don't think you're in any position to be joking."

"I figure you knew Miguel back in Argentina."

"Yes. We go back a long way," he answered, his voice full of anger but accented with an undertone of sentimentality.

"What do you want from him?" I asked, wanting to draw him in, hoping to distract him long enough to make a move.

"The same thing you do. To see justice done. Let's just say our interests are now aligned."

"Why have me go to Montreal? Why not wait till he comes back?"

"I need to know who he's meeting. I'll pay for your expenses at your going rate. If what you find doesn't pique your interest, we'll go our separate ways."

"Well, I hate to break it to you. Even if I wanted to cut a deal, I'm still a wanted felon."

"I left a gift for you in the trunk of your caddy. It should help clear things up with the authorities."

"How's that?"

But there was no answer. The pressure in my back was also gone. I turned cautiously but saw no sign of the mysterious assailant. I headed to my caddy, keeping a cautious eye open in case this was a trap. I met none.

I popped the caddy's trunk. I found the thug who killed Miss Stonewall hogtied and ready for roasting. His mouth was gagged with a dirty piece of cloth I had lying about in the trunk. But he was still breathing.

A folded piece of paper was pinned to his coat's lapel. He stirred as I leaned in to retrieve it, and our eyes met. They shone with dread and horror like he had confronted his greatest fear. And I was sure it wasn't me. But I wondered what it took to instill such fear in a hardened killer.

Unfolding the note, I discovered a handwritten confession by the thug, confessing his part in the murder of Stonewall—how he had framed me and where he had dumped her body. I called Ant. This time, I waited.

36

YOU'RE TELLING ME you've no idea who this guy is?" Ant asked. I was in his office, awaiting the slow grind of bureaucracy to finish the paperwork that would make me a free man again.

"None. It's the first time I've come across him."

"And he says the Fox is in Montreal and wants you to go after him?"

"Not go after him exactly. Just find out who he's meeting with."

"But I can have the Montreal Police do that, even arrest him—"

"And charge him with what? We've got nothing on him except the kidnapping charge. And you know what happened last time. And there'd be the whole extradition process that could take months or years."

"You've got a point there. But are you seriously considering the advice of a psychopath who was ready to shred you?"

"He didn't, though. He wants Fox as badly as we do. Besides, he's offered us a huge lead that might at least shed light on Miguel's true motivation behind the heist."

"I still think this is a bad idea."

"I don't think we have a choice. We need solid proof and quick. Before it's too late."

"But why'd this guy bring you into his confidence? What's in it for him?" Ant asked.

"That's a good question I've been juggling inside my head. There are two possibilities. One, he's setting me up as a patsy for something."

"With the Fox pulling the strings," Ant added.

"Exactly. But that doesn't jive. Why would Miguel play it that way?"

"Maybe he's looking to finish you there?"

"If he wanted me dead, the stranger could have done that."

"Right."

"Which brings me to the second possibility."

"Which is?"

"That the stranger is on the level."

"But how do you know you can trust him?"

"I don't. But he left me that gift in the trunk of my caddy. Whatever reason he had, we must follow through. It's all we got."

Ant mulled this over for a few minutes.

"Alright, James, the paperwork should be done within the next hour. I hope you know what you're doing."

"Me too."

I phoned Piña while waiting for my newfound freedom. She seemed relieved and happy for me, but I still sensed a particular reservation in her voice. She was also in a hurry. She was flying back to Chicago in a couple of hours. I asked if I could drive her to the airport. She agreed.

She was waiting for me outside her hotel when I pulled up. She gave me a long, lingering kiss as soon as she got in. I didn't object. But tears had swelled across her eyes when she finally pulled away. I hated such moments—those long goodbyes.

"I'll miss you, James."

"Hey, we'll see each other real soon. You're only a couple of hours away by car."

"You promise?"

"I promise," I said, hoping it sounded sincere. She gave me a penetrating stare, questioning our future.

"I'm so sorry to hear about Sangria," she said.

"Yeah, that was a bad break. The guy was a pain, but he was growing on me. Any word on Sam?"

"None. I don't know how much longer she can last on her own. It's not like she's some rodent. She'd be conspicuous anywhere she went."

"I agree." But she caught the hint of doubt in my voice.

"You don't think she's dead, do you?"

"We can't rule it out. As you said, someone should have spotted her by now. But there is the other possibility."

"Which is?"

"What Miss Stonewall first suggested. She is being held captive?"

"To what end?"

"Another puzzle amongst many. The case is some sort of Rubik's Cube. If I could only shift the pieces to their proper positions, everything would click into place."

"I hope you're right, James."

"Me too," I said, having echoed the exact sentiments hours earlier to Ant. But a sense of foreboding now overshadowed my determination—like a distant storm on the horizon. After dropping Piña off, I got on the i94 and headed to my next destination— Montreal.

37

MIGUEL SAT PATIENTLY in his luxury suite at the Ritz-Carlton in Montreal, waiting for his visitors to arrive. His suite went for seven hundred per night, but money was no object. The group that invited him was footing the bill.

This wasn't the only time Miguel had met them. The first time was in Buenos Aires several years earlier. He knew them only by their aliases—appropriated from Greek mythology.

For example, there was Ares, the god of war, and Artemis, the goddess of the moon and the hunt. And Hypnos, the god of sleep. They honored Miguel with the namesake, Hades, the god of death and the underworld.

Miguel thought the group's seven members—pompous and overzealous. Their arrogance annoyed him. The group believed they possessed the power and resources to change the world—to fashion it into a utopian new order of their making.

Little did they know their divine presence would soon become a footnote to Miguel's self-tailored mythology.

Zero, at first, wasn't sure what to make of Cartwright. He knew that intimidation and fear wouldn't work on him. Not because Cartwright was above such approaches—everyone had their breaking point. But because he figured Cartwright to be highly principled and lived by a moral code like himself. And it was through these mutual values he saw the best chance of convincing Cartwright to join forces, even if it was only temporary.

Zero could have taken Miguel out on his own. That was his original intent until he learned about a meeting between Miguel and some nefarious group and a private eye: hounding Miguel with the help of an Interpol Agent.

So, he decided to change strategies and approach the PI about Montreal. If the PI took him up on his offer, he'd stay back, preparing for Miguel's return.

38

IT WASN'T MY FIRST TRIP to Canada. Several years back, I came to the aid of an ex-partner and friend of mine, Shelby Mercer, who had moved to Toronto. He'd been framed for the murder of a dirty cop. I eventually exonerated Mercer by figuring out the cop's son had done the killing.

I had just passed the city of Kingston, about a three-hour jaunt southwest of Montreal. I decided to stop for gas and something to eat. Plus, I'd picked up a tail along the way. They were in a nondescript, dark, navy-blue Chevy four-door. They were good at their job since spotting them had taken me this long. I had to assume that they'd been tailing me since the border. My hunch was that they were probably feds—Canadian, maybe American. I wasn't sure. I'd have to lose them at some point, but for now, I was starving.

Parking the caddy, I made my way to the fast-food chain restaurant for a burger and fries. The great thing about these chains was that they made you feel like you'd never left the U.S. of A. The food was exactly the same.

I thought navigating Montreal's streets wouldn't differ much from that of Toronto or the Motor City. But I was sadly mistaken. I realized it the moment I crossed the Ontario border into Quebec.

The welcome sign read *Bienvenue* on a large, free-standing structure painted blue and white—the official colors of the province.

It wasn't necessarily the language that tripped me up as much as the maze of roads and haphazard placement of signs. They seemed to appear at the last minute, forcing me to retrace my route several times. I'm sure once one got used to it all, it'd become second nature, but it was highway hell for a rookie like me.

The tail I had picked up earlier was still with me. They probably thought that the way I was driving, I was trying to lose them. A stupid grin crossed my face at the thought.

I finally arrived at the BNB I had booked, located on Sherbrooke St., a few blocks east of St. Denis. Once again, I had a hell of a time deciphering the parking signs. There were a half dozen lining the street with contradictory instructions.

One sign claimed that you could park between 10 am and 2 pm, while another stated that parking was with a permit only. I finally gave up and parked in front of the BNB, where another sign read, No Stopping.

As I checked into the BNB, I asked the attendant what I should do about parking. He smiled sympathetically and told me he couldn't help since he didn't drive. He suggested I park on Sherbrooke, where metered parking was available. He'd ask the manager about it when he came in at six.

My room was on the second floor. It was small but comfortable, with a twin bed, a small writing desk and plenty of light streaming through. I dropped my travel bag on the bed and headed right back down.

I asked the clerk where the Ritz-Carlton was located. Fear riddled his eyes, believing I was unsatisfied with the accommodation. I eased his fears immediately, explaining I was to meet a friend there.

"Oui, Monsieur. Just go west on Sherbrooke Ave. It's about a ten-minute drive."

"And west being—"

"Once you exit the building, go to your left."

"Merci," I said, one of the few French words I knew.

"Ça m'a fait plaisir," he returned.

39

THE GROUP ARRIVED punctually at two. Miguel sat in an oversized brown leather chair, nursing his glass of scotch and observing the proceedings with amusement as each member took their place at the round conference table.

When he first met the group, he demanded they use a round table. He explained that in this way, no one appeared more important than the other, as was the case during King Arthur's times.

Miguel was amused by the scenario because the issue of which of them was Arthur never came up. Most likely, each imagined themselves in the role.

Now seated at their respective places, Miguel begrudgingly got up, sitting between Hermes and Dionysus. The Group of Seven became eight.

"Let the meeting begin," announced an overweight man whose double chin would have given a wild turkey a run for its money. He was known to the group as Ares, *the god of war and bloodshed*. And the name suited him well. His stock in trade was the sale of arms to the highest bidder. Miguel detested him. If experience had taught him anything, it was only to trust people with a sense of duty or morality.

"I concur," came the reply from Demeter, *goddess of the harvest and fertility*. She was of slender build, well-proportioned, and eyes that radiated like a distant star. Miguel figured she'd led many an unsuspecting lover to their demise.

Aphrodite, a voluptuous redhead who Miguel figured to be in her sixties, but didn't look a day over forty, seconded the request. Miguel found it absurd that everyone was here to discuss the planet's destruction but insisted on such formalities.

"All right then, let's begin with you, Hades," Ares said. All attention turned to Miguel. "Have you been in touch with the doctor?"

Ares was referring to Miguel's friend Dr. Emanuel Degas, who engineered the virus.

"Yes, I have. I'm to meet with him later today."

"What? He's here! In Montreal?" came the boisterous voice of Zeus. "Do you think that's wise, Hades?"

"No. I agree, but he insisted. How did he put it? Oh, yes... he wanted to see the fall of the capitalist pigs and their corpses burn in hell with his own eyes. His very words."

"I see," Zeus said, calming down a bit. "Does this mean he intends to travel back with you to the States?"

"Yes, that's the plan."

"And what of the virus's progress?" Hermes, *the messenger of the gods and guide to dead souls*, asked eagerly.

The guy was too much of a ghoul for Miguel's taste. He seemed to thrive on others' misfortune. Dressed immaculately in what one could only describe as a funeral director's attire—a black wool tailored suit, white pressed cotton shirt and a thin tie with a perfect hand knot, accentuated by his hollowed-out eyes and thin frame—he played his role to a tee.

"Yes, the virus," Miguel answered, pausing momentarily to consider what to tell them. "Well, according to the good doctor and the statistics published by WHO, the infection rate is close to three percent of the population."

"But surely that's not enough for the plan to work? Hermes protested.

"Perhaps not for your ghoulish tastes," Miguel countered, "but enough to cause an economic meltdown and worldwide panic."

"I must agree with Hermes," Zeus interjected. "If we are to make our plan a reality, the virus must infect a much larger portion of the population. We can introduce our pure bloodlines once the masses can no longer procreate. Then all will be as it should be."

"I also agree with Hermes and Zeus," Aphrodite said. "This is what we agreed upon when we put our plan in motion. Or have you reconsidered, Hades?"

"I never agreed to or entertained such beliefs. Joining the group was only to satisfy my desire—to see Argentina in all its glory again. I don't care what happens to the rest of the world. It's all yours for the taking," Miguel countered.

"It's true what Hades says." It was Demeter coming to Miguel's aid. "He made it quite clear from the beginning why he joined us. We respect that. But what of the virus, Hades? Does the doctor believe we can reach our goal?"

"He believes that before the scientific community deciphers its true intention, it will have infected twenty percent of the population. That translates to over one point five billion humans becoming infertile."

"It's strange to think," Athena added, who remained silent until now. "It took over two-hundred thousand years for humans to have a population of a billion souls, but over the past two hundred years, we've reached almost eight billion."

"Well, that definitely will be a thing of the past," Zeus interjected. "That's why the success of the plan is so important. We must alter the inevitable fate that threatens our species."

Why, so humanity can experience an even more horrible fate under your guise, Miguel was tempted to add. But this was not the time. He had other plans for the group. And it was already in play.

40

I HEADED WEST along Sherbrooke, as the desk clerk had suggested. In the early 1700s, this part of the city was known as *The Baron Hillside* for all the mansions that occupied the area. The street was popular with the wealthy due in part to its distance from the working-class residents who settled along the banks of the St. Lawrence River below.

Sherbrooke sat on the plateau's edge, where the elite could look down on their subjects. The plateau spread north toward Mont-Royal, a small mountain that rose from the city's core, from which the city of Montreal took its name.

A one-hundred-and-three-foot steel cross sat on the mountain's peak—the original was made of wood and erected back in 1642 by De Maisonneuve, one of the city's co-founders. Supposedly, he prayed to the Virgin Mary, pleading that she spared the city from the onslaught of a devastating flood. It seems his prayers had paid off.

Finally reaching my destination, I parked the caddy and paid the exorbitant street meter fees. The Ritz-Carlton was first opened in 1912, designed by the architects who also designed Grand Central Station in

New York. The list of rich and famous that graced the hotel's walls was impressive.

During the '20s, movie stars like Mary Pickford and Douglas Fairbanks stayed there, followed by Winston Churchill, Charles de Gaulle, Marlene Dietrich, and Liberace.

In the '60s, when Howard Hughes visited the city, he booked most of the eighth floor for himself. Elizabeth Taylor and Richard Burton got hitched here. In '71, Richard Nixon booked a suite during his visit. And in '72, The Rolling Stones were denied entrance to its dining lodge until they returned with the appropriate attire.

The hotel went through three major renovations, the latest back in 2012. So, I doubted I'd get the sense of the excitement and grandeur of those gone-by years.

But Miguel may have thought differently. Perhaps, this was why he chose the place, to get in touch with and rekindle his past glory. But I figured his stay was more sinister than misguided vanity.

I approached the door attendant guarding the revolving doors in front. He was an elderly gentleman, outfitted in a black service hat, a long suit overcoat and black slacks. He was eyeing my approach like an exterminator does their prey.

"Good day, sir," he announced as I neared him. "How can I be of service?"

"I heard that an old friend was staying at your venerable establishment. I was coming to see if he was still around."

"Around, sir?" He threw back with a hint of old English in his voice. "And who might that be?"

"His name's Miguel Peterson," I said, lying about Miguel's last name. "He's about five feet, five inches tall, well dressed, and uses a silver-tipped cane to get around."

"Sounds more like a suspect than a friend, if you ask me, sir."

"You got me there," I said, giving up any attempt to deceive him. I pulled out my PI license and handed it to him.

"A private detective. Really. From the United States. What kind?"

"Kind?"

"Yes. What kind of detecting do you do, sir? Infidelity, fraud, corporate espionage. There are so many unsavory elements that plague our society today."

I wasn't sure if he was being serious or pulling my leg, but I played along. "Well, I usually investigate the most unsavory of all crimes, that of murder."

"Really, and you suspect your friend of such a deed?" he asked, now sporting a smirk.

"He isn't exactly a friend, as I'm sure you've already surmised. But I must know his whereabouts. I shouldn't tell you this, but it's a matter of national security." I figured this pitch always worked for the Feds, so why not give it a go?

"Whose nation?" he asked, still toying with me.

I was tired of playing his cat-and-mouse game, so I chose a different tactic. "All nations," I said, adding a hint of anger and frustration for good measure. "You know about this virus that's going around?" He nodded in the affirmative. "Well, it turns out that this guy may be behind its spread." His grin was gone, and his attention was glued to my every word. "So, it's a matter of life and death that we track this individual," I added, pushing to my advantage.

"I just don't know..."

"Listen!" I cut in, pushing harder. "I'm just a servant like yourself doing his job. Help me out."

He pondered this for a hard minute as he looked nervously around him. Finally, he said, "Yes. He booked in early this morning."

"Any idea which room?"

"695."

"OK. Thanks. I'll let the authorities know that you were very cooperative."

"I'd appreciate that. Thank you, sir." I moved through the revolving doors, leaving the door attendant to consider what had just hit him.

The hotel was spacious and adorned with marble walls and elaborate gold-painted trim. Only a handful of guests were mulling around and less busy than expected. Probably had something to do with the virus. I bought a copy of the New York Times from the hotel's gift shop. Then I headed to one of the lobby's tanned leather sofa chairs, which offered an unobstructed view of the elevators. I sat and waited.

41

THE GROUP OF SEVEN finally left. Miguel poured himself a double shot of scotch, then picked up the phone on the credenza, dialed a number and waited for a response.

"Pronto," the voice on the other end said.

"It's me, Miguel. They've left. You can come by now."

Seconds later, there was a knock on the door. Miguel went to open it. Dr. Emanuel Degas was standing outside his door.

"Come in, my friend," Miguel said, excited. He grabbed Emanuel's hand like a kid does their mother's—dragging her to a hidden treasure they'd discovered.

"Piacere anche di rivederti, amico mio," Emanuel said, also excited to see Miguel.

"What would you like to drink? I have everything, as you can see," waving his arms around him. "The fools are paying for it all."

"Some grappa, if you have it."

"Yes. Coming right up."

Miguel moved to the bar in search of the requested drink from the extensive selection of liquors. Finally spotting it, he poured a generous amount into a long-stemmed tulip glass. Returning to Emanuel, he handed him his drink. He sat next to him on the black leather couch positioned in front of a large arched window that gave a panoramic view of the city's skyline to the south, along the St. Lawrence River.

"Salute," Emanuel said.

"Salute," Miguel returned, clicking his glass with Emanuel's.

After taking a moment to savor his drink, Emanuel said, "Did you know that Grappa was once a poor man's drink."

"No, I didn't."

"Yes. It's distilled from what's left over from the precious grapes used to make wine. The pulp, seeds, and stems are all used. Its fragrance differs depending on the grapes."

"Always the chemist, my friend," Miguel said, smiling.

"What else is there? We are, after all, chromosomal abnormalities subject to the chemical aberrations around us, water, air, earth..."

"So, it boils down to the fact that we're all test subjects at the mercy of some evolutionary power we have no control over."

"Exactly. And if we were ever to harness these powers, well, we would be as gods," Emanuel added with a wide manic grin.

"Speaking of power and evolution, when do you think the virus will reach critical mass?" Miguel asked, wanting to shift the conversation to the business at hand,

"As I told you earlier, it has infected at least three percent of the population. According to my calculations, hitting the ten percent marker should take another week. Then there's no turning back."

"And the vaccine will work?"

"Yes, providing it's released before the virus reaches ten percent. After that, the damage will be too widespread for the vaccine to do any good."

"Then we mustn't waste any time contacting the proper authorities and negotiating a hefty price for the vaccine," Miguel said, excited.

"I thought this was all about restoring Argentina to its former days," Emanuel asked, his voice trembling, his face etched with concern. "And making the Americans pay for their arrogance and intrusion into our affairs."

"Yes, yes, of course, it is," Miguel answered, trying to reassure his friend. "But the only thing the Americans understand is money. Now that their financial establishments are in crisis because of the virus, we can bend them to our will. And as for that righteous Group," pointing toward the door from which the Group of Seven had left, "are you sure the fake vaccine we gave them will work?"

"I'm sure. By taking that batch, they'll be directly infecting themselves and their followers with a similar strain of the virus, which has no vaccine. The days of propagating their kind are over."

"Excellent.

"But Miguel, is it right to play God with all these people's lives? Are we not repeating the horrors of the past? All those deaths and hardships caused by the coups and revolutions, I'd never want that to happen again."

"Not at all, my friend. That is why you made the virus to maim and not kill. Yes, there were mistakes made in the past. You lost your son in all that madness. But this is different. We must stop those fanatics like the Group—wanting to clone a world into their likeness. If we don't, Argentina, as we know it, and love will cease to exist. There would only be one country, one state—theirs."

"But why did you ask me to create the virus for them in the first place?"

"I wanted to control the outcome. Someone would inevitably use such drastic means to gain power. We live in precarious times."

"But I still don't fully understand your end game."

"It's simple. Cripple the forces that drive the world's economy. Without an economy, without money, their power dissipates. I want to press the reset switch."

Emanuel looked long and hard into his friend's face. Dread and uncertainty filled his soul. He wanted to believe in the cause but knew things never happened as they should. If that were the case, his son would still be alive.

But he loved Miguel with all his heart. And he would travel to hell and back for him. He moved in close and planted a long and passionate kiss on his lips. Miguel reciprocated. They then got up and moved into the luxurious bedroom across the room, shutting the door behind them.

42

AN HOUR HAD PASSED since I sat down. So far, nothing. No sign of Miguel or any suspicious activity. The flow of check-ins was at an all-time low. People were taking the virus seriously, having decided against travel. It didn't help that Canada had also placed a moratorium on international travel, allowing entry to the country only for essential personnel. Thanks to Ant, I was one of the chosen few.

I had read the paper cover to cover. The news, as usual, made me want to stick my head in a gas oven. There were the expected headlines, such as the continuing conflict in the Middle East and plans to impeach the U.S. president over corruption, which wasn't news based on his track record.

Also, the Antarctic had reached a balmy sixty-five degrees matching that of Los Angeles. Argentina was renegotiating its fifty-seven-billion-dollar debt owed to the International Monetary Fund. Its inflation rate was about to hit a whopping fifty-four percent.

But most of the news focused on the spread of the virus. To date, it had infected over a hundred and fifty million people worldwide, killing over two-hundred thousand people. Scientists and politicians cautioned people not to panic, that the fatality rate was low, comparable to that of the flu. That was easy for them to say. It wasn't their asses on the line.

What was most disconcerting for the scientists was that they still hadn't figured out the source of the virus. There were rampant rumors that its origin was alien. But equally hypothesized was the possibility someone genetically engineered it. The last option bothered me the most. It was one thing for nature to wreak havoc on us for not respecting its domain, but to unleash a plague with deliberate malice—well, that was just sick. But not surprising.

I counted between twenty to twenty-five guests roaming the lobby during my watch. There was a young couple I assumed to be newlyweds, judging by their naïve joy at the world around them. And why wouldn't they feel that way? They had their entire life ahead of them.

Then there was a woman wearing a tight-fitting, red leather dress accented by a plume of peacock feathers wrapped along her neckline strutting around with the tallest pair of silver pumps I'd ever seen. She also had the figure and looks to pull it off.

But what really piqued my interest was a group of business executives who had just exited the elevators. They had congregated around the front desk and were checking out, having handed in their key cards. They were also all carrying similar brown leather attaché cases. I got up and moved to the travel brochure stand a few feet from the check-out counter. I was far enough away to not attract any immediate attention but close enough to eavesdrop on their conversation.

"The old man has become a problem," I heard the one with the double chin say.

"I agree," said the woman next to him. She wore a smart-looking, blue-gray business suit that must have cost her a working stiff's yearly salary. Then looking around nervously, she added, "We must do something about it."

"We'll discuss it in more detail once we get back," the man on the other side of her interjected in a stern voice. He looked like he'd be a shoo-in for a funeral director. The four executives right behind the three nodded in agreement. They then turned and walked in unison, like a colony of army ants, through the hotel's revolving front doors.

I decided not to follow, having spotted the hotel's extensive surveillance system earlier. I'd get Ant to extract the feed and reveal their identities through facial recognition. But for now, the priority was Miguel's whereabouts.

ORANGUTAN

43

PIÑA WAS HAVING trouble breathing. The humid air generated by the oppressive heat was unbearable. The poignant smell of rotting vegetation, flowers, and dirt, further added to her distress.

Looking up, she could make out splintered rays of sunlight trying hard to push through the dense canopy surrounding her. Droplets of rain were filtering down, tree by tree, leaf by leaf, toward her.

Some hit their intended destination while others insisted on perfecting their drip torture technique—slamming against her forehead, then bouncing hard to the ground. She kept swiping and cursing at them but to no avail.

Piña knew precisely where she was. She had spent most of her youth exploring the Amazon rainforest in her native Ecuador.

But there was something different this time. She felt like a stranger in a place she had once considered home. She couldn't quite put her finger on why. She wasn't sure if it was the smells, the feel and look, or the strange shimmering light blanketing the forest. Or the sounds that were more intense than how she remembered them—the irregular chirping of birds, the clicks and buzzing of the cicadas, and the croaking of frogs. Whatever it was, she could feel her anxiety rising.

And she was sure she was being watched. A sharp recoil from the undergrowth behind verified her suspicions. She swung around, locking with a pair of amber eyes peering out from behind the large ferns. She'd recognize those eyes anywhere.

"Sam?" she asked excitedly.

Sam responded immediately, pushing through into the clearing, her fists propelling her forward. She stopped several feet from Piña and let out a sharp hissing noise followed by a series of low, drawn-out sounds through her nostrils as a welcome.

"How are you, Sam?" Piña asked out loud and gesturing her question through sign language—shaping her hands into arches, connected at the knuckles and bringing them up against her chest. She then rolled them down in front of her, her palms still cupped and open, toward Sam while raising her eyebrows.

Sam responded by stamping the ground and pushing out her lower lip. She was also happy to see Piña and immediately followed up with another gesture. She wanted Piña to follow her.

"Where to?" Piña asked.

But Sam ignored her, turning and stomping off in the direction she had come from. Piña followed. After ten minutes of maneuvering through the thick underbrush, Piña heard running water. She assumed its source was from one of the hundreds of tributaries flowing from the Amazon River.

Sure enough, five minutes later, she stood with Sam along the shore of a small river around two-hundred feet wide—its rapids pushing hard downstream—violent and deadly.

Sam lifted his arm, motioning for Piña to look upriver. At first, she saw nothing. But a dark speck on the horizon gradually came into view.

It was moving toward her. The closer it got, the more bizarre the possibility of what she was witnessing became.

Now only about a hundred yards off, the speck turned out to be a man on a large raft caught in the fast-moving rapids. And if the sighting wasn't strange enough, he was also dressed as a Spanish conquistador.

He wore a *cabasset* helmet made of steel and cap-shaped into an elongated dome, its peak looking like the tip of an almond. It covered his head from the ears up. He also donned an *escuapil*, a padded leather amour adapted from the Aztec warriors.

But this still wasn't the strangest part of the sighting. With his three-foot narrow sword, the conquistador desperately tried to fend off a troop of monkeys surrounding him on the raft. For every ape he killed, two would take their place.

As Piña watched him pass her, their eyes met. His eyes were bursting with blood-red rage. She knew without a doubt he'd gone mad. But that was a moot point. Within minutes he'd hit the falls up ahead, never to be seen again.

"Hello, Piña. Remember me." A voice from behind her asked.

Even before facing the voice, she knew who it belonged to. It was Allan Abner, the assistant suspected of making off with the gems in the pink pig. He wore the same clothing the night he was murdered, complete with a blood-soaked bullet wound in his upper chest. Blood was gushing out from it.

"What are you doing here?" She asked, angered and disturbed by his presence but not necessarily surprised by his appearance.

"I'm here to collect."

"Collect what?"

"You know very well what."

"No, I don't…" but she couldn't complete her sentence. A deafening buzz began to increase in volume and intensity.

Opening her eyes, she realized her alarm clock had gone off. The red LED lights were telling her it was 2:30 in the morning.

Still shaken from her dream, she forced herself out of bed and threw on a pair of track pants and a loosely fitting blouse. Then grabbing her backpack, she headed out the door.

44

IT WAS ONE in the morning before I got back from Montreal, with a plethora of thoughts rattling inside my head. I had now increased the list of suspects from three to eleven, which was ass-backward. The idea was to eliminate suspects, not add more.

First, there was the Fox, who wasn't so much a suspect as a sure bet and wanted fugitive, with enough evidence to put him away for life—if one could ever catch him. Then there was the older man I saw leaving with Miguel and the group of seven business executives I eavesdropped on while they were checking out of the hotel. And to top that list off, there was the lawyer who was most likely instrumental in Sangria's death and the pale stranger who tipped me off about Montreal.

I was exhausted—my head was ready to explode. I threw back a few shots of bourbon, inhaled a half dozen smokes, and turned on the TV—blitzing out on those infomercials that usually haunt the TV waves at that hour. Finally, I dozed off.

Four orangutans were circling me. They appeared angry about something—stomping their fists on the ground, accompanied by loud grumphs, causing the ground below to thunder. Their eyes were lit up like nuggets of black coal, like some inferno. I wasn't sure what I had done to anger the beasts besides perhaps trespassing on their sacred space, which was a damn good reason in my books. And just when I thought *I was done for, this is it, there's no way out*, a voice from behind shouted, "Stop!"

I turned to confront the voice only to find Piña standing there, cloaked in a white ceremonial gown, her arm outstretched, her palm open and directed toward the orangutans. They had obeyed, abruptly stopping their dance of death. Now still and silent, they awaited further instructions from their master.

"Piña, what are you doing here? What's happening?" I asked. But got no answer. She was focused on the wall behind me that held the remaining twenty glyphs. Again, the glyphs glowed as they slid off the wall like furtive shadows, moving quickly and determinedly along the floor toward her. When they were only within inches away, she gestured with a sweeping upward motion of her arm and open palm. The glyphs reacted at once. They moved along the surface of her legs, under her gown and up to her arms and face, etching themselves into her skin along the way.

"Now we are one," she said.

The four orangutans that had surrounded me became excited about this latest development. They began pounding their fists even more violently than before, breaking into a primal dance accompanied by the uttering of a multitude of expressive grunts—obviously, a language that I was not privy to.

I looked on in abject horror, feeling utterly helpless to do anything. And just when I thought the whole thing couldn't get any weirder, Piña started transforming. Now glowing a bright red, her face and body began shapeshifting into an oversized fox.

At first, she seemed confused, eyeing me inquisitively, wondering how she had gotten there and who I was. But a moment later, burst into laughter—laughter so manic and piercing I jammed my hands against my ears to block it. But it didn't help.

The laughter was already in me, inside my head, permeating through my entire body. I felt myself shaking uncontrollably, in sync with its demonic vibrations—my body being torn apart.

Then without notice, it all stopped. Piña and her ape friends were gone. I was back in my bedroom. The small portable black-and-white TV was still on, its ghoulish rays irradiating everything in its path. A rerun of *Back to the Future* was playing.

45

ZERO CLIMBED THE LONG, narrow stairs until he reached a reinforced steel door. He pressed the illuminated button next to it and looked up at the surveillance camera pointed toward him. A buzzer rang, followed by the sound of the door's locking mechanisms being released.

Once through the door, he made his way down a narrower hallway than the one he had navigated coming up the stairs. This led him to the five-foot stainless-steel counter with a plated glass shield that reached up to the ceiling.

A young man with a muscular build wearing a white cut-off muscle t-shirt and a pair of blue sweatpants was busying himself, folding bleach-white towels.

Zero tapped the small knob on the domed silver bell on the counter. The man twisted his neck around to see who it was and asked, "Locker or room?"

"Room," Zero answered in a dry monotone voice.

"Four hours or the entire night?" the attendant then asked.

"What are the rates?" Zero asked in return.

"Twenty bucks for four, thirty for the night."

"I'll take the night," he said, deciding on the spur of the moment.

He wasn't sure how long it would take to carry out his task. He handed the attendant the required fee, who then passed him one of the recently folded towels and a transparent, glossy red packet containing a condom from the fishbowl sitting on the counter. Then passing Zero the key to his room, the attendant offered a conspiratorial smile and pressed a button hidden below the counter. The door next to him buzzed, and Zero pushed through, but not before stealing a glance back. The attendant had returned to his folding. He wondered what was so fascinating about the towels that held the attendant's unwavering attention.

It took a moment for Zero's eyes to adjust to the dimly lit interior. Besides, the place was like a maze. He had to navigate half-a-dozen corridors before finding his room. Along the way, he was propositioned several times but politely excused himself, saying he was there to meet someone. Finally finding his room, he inserted the key the attendant gave him into the door lock marked No.9.

The room was small, measuring only six by eight feet. The smell of body odor and expired sex dripped off its walls. It was a smell he was familiar with.

He quickly stripped, wrapped the towel around his waist, and left the room for the showers. Fortunately, no one was around, and he could enjoy the shower in solitude. Once done, he dried himself lightly, wrapping the towel once again around his waist and returned to his room.

He unzipped the black leather backpack that he brought with him. It was sitting on the floor next to the cot he hoped had been fumigated at least once in the past few weeks.

Pulling out the pack's contents, he laid them carefully in a row onto the bed. There was a strawberry red wig, a black bra and panties made of lace, black silk stockings, and garter belts. The last item he pulled out was a pair of ruby red stiletto high heels, placing them next to the other items.

He took a few moments to contemplate his treasures before opening the small make-up bag he had also brought. From it, he pulled out a small mirror, a tube of ruby-red lipstick, black eyeliner, and other accessories he'd require to complete his appearance.

It had been several years since he last cross-dressed. And he missed it. Initially, it helped relieve his anxiety over the constant demand for his machismo appearance.

The macho thing had been good for business, especially with the hard-cold persona he had incorporated into his act. But soon, he'd be finished with that life. Realize his true destiny.

He remembered what the Renaissance sculptor Michelangelo once said: *I saw the angel in the marble and carved until I set it free*. That's what he was doing —setting himself free.

This was the other reason he'd come to the States, to see a doctor about starting treatments. The process would be expensive, but that wouldn't be a problem after tonight.

Zero wondered how the private eye he sent to Montreal had fared. He didn't expect much would come of it but was still curious about who Miguel was meeting. He'd contact Cartwright tomorrow. By then, he'd have finished his business here.

46

TALK OF THE VIRUS was front and center on every new channel and talk show. World leaders, including leading scientists, were making frequent press conferences, suggesting ways to stop its spread. Suggestions included shutting everything down to the mandatory wearing of masks. Some said such measures were draconian, and others argued enough wasn't being done. Conspiracy theories were rampant, some claiming it was the end times while others blamed the new Wi-Fi technology for its origin and transmission.

"It's just too much," Elvis protested as he got up to turn off his sixty-inch flat-screen monitor.

"What? That your TV takes up more than a third of your room," I said, ribbing him. Elvis occupied a one-bedroom apartment with a small kitchenette and living room that doubled as his office and entertainment center.

"Funny guy. Are you ever going to stop bitching about the screen? I need it for my leisure time. I want to feel immersed in whatever I'm doing. That's why I also have these killer headphones I plug into when

I'm alone. I can blast the sound as loud as I want till hell freezes over, and no one can tell me otherwise."

"Is that true for the virus? Do you want to catch it to have an immersive experience?"

"Don't kid around about those things, James. This is serious, and we've got a punk in power who wouldn't even know if the Russians invaded us until it was too late."

"But what's he supposed to do? Shut down the whole country?"

"Yeah. That's exactly what he's supposed to do."

"And what about the economy, the millions of jobs people depend on to survive?"

"It's about short-term pain for long-term gain, James. Plus, he could offer compensation to the people hardest hit, like they're doing up in Canada?"

"You got a point there. It would make sense to stop this thing before it gets out of hand. But I've got a feeling it may already be too late."

"What about the vaccine? They say they're close," Elvis said, excited about the prospect.

"Could be, but from what I've heard, they don't even know the virus's origin or what it's doing to those that catch it. Could be years before they have a vaccine that works."

"And you still figure Fox is behind it?"

"The more I uncover, the more I'm becoming a believer. The coincidences and patterns dictate that logically, it must be so."

"Whoa. I just got this strange Trek vibe. You know, James, all that logic and rationale you hold dear has its limits. That's why you always need a Captain Kirk to balance out the game."

"And what, are you vying for Kirk's position?"

"Why not? I figure I'd make a great Kirk. Plus, I'd have no problem navigating the final frontier—going where no Motor City resident has before."

We both broke out in laughter. It was good to be laughing again. Not since my date with Piña a few days back had I felt any hope left in the world.

"So, you'll put the word out on the street about this killer roaming the streets and let me know when you have something."

"As soon as I got something, I'll let you know, James. Until then, keep safe."

"You too, my friend." .

47

THE LAST TIME I had so much trouble sleeping was seven years ago. I had failed to talk down a very upset and emotional seventeen-year-old with a gun. She ended up killing her mother. It wasn't my fault—that's what everyone told me. And they were right. It wasn't on me to change who people are. But I couldn't shake the sense of guilt and failure.

I told my doctor about my sleeping problem, hoping he'd prescribe some magical pills. But leave it to me to end up with an ethical doc. He demanded I see someone before prescribing anything. So, on his recommendation, I met with Dr. Amelia Adams.

The last thing I thought I'd do was see a shrink. I was old school and didn't feel comfortable seeking help from others, especially with my personal life. I had a priest for that. But it'd been over fifteen years since I felt a completion to confess.

But the doctor turned out to be an extraordinary person. Her charm and demeanor won me over right off. She didn't push any psychobabble on me. She just let me figure it all out at my pace.

So, I decided to turn to her once again. These bizarre dreams I'd been having of late were getting to me.

"So nice to see you again, James," she said in a steady and raspy voice, with the overtones of Janis Joplin or an Edith Piaf.

She could have been quite an accomplished singer if she had decided to move in that direction. But selfishly, I was glad she hadn't. At the time, we had become a bit too close, with the possibility of our professional relationship developing into something more. But nothing happened. This was a good thing since I'd be left with no one I could trust to exorcise my demons.

"Nice to see you as well, Dr. Adams. Thanks for making time for me on such short notice."

"No problem, James. You phoned me just at the right time. I had a cancellation." I wasn't sure if that was entirely true. "But I'm sorry to hear you're having trouble sleeping again," wrinkles of concern shadowing her pale, oval face—which reminded me of a Modigliani painting. "So, tell me about these dreams of yours?"

I told her about the three dreams. She listened intently without interruption. When I finally finished, she said, more as a statement than a question, "You're on a case, aren't you?"

"When am I not?" I said, offering a faint and tired smile.

"I ask because of the heavy symbolism in your dreams. It seems you're trying to work out serious issues that require answers. You may already have them, but your conscious mind refuses to accept them."

"You got that all from what I told you."

"Not everything. But don't forget I got to know you during our other sessions, which gives me a head start on what's happening."

"Kind of scary," I said, sounding slightly defensive but trying to make light of it. "I can't imagine your analysis if you had the full picture."

"It's not like that, James. No one can ever know everything about someone. Not even themselves. There are so many factors at play. All we can hope for is a glimpse of the direction we should be moving toward."

"So, what you're saying, is that we're all damned." Her face lit up at my last comment.

"You know, that's one of your most pervasive defense mechanisms. Trying to make light of difficult situations. Which I can't blame you for. You must see horrific things."

"It comes with the territory."

"Yes. I'm sure it does," she said, peering deep into my eyes, hoping to capture one of those nuggets of insight she mentioned earlier.

But I figured she got nothing for her troubles since she cut back with, "So, about these dreams, you've been having."

"Any ideas?"

"A few. Let's examine them individually, which may give us a bigger picture."

"Sounds good."

"But first, let me ask you. This case you're on, it's got you stumped?"

"Yeah. It's like a riddle wrapped in an enigma wrapped in —you know. I just can't get a handle on it. Every time I figure I'm close, something else drops, derailing those assumptions."

"Perhaps that's the problem. It sounds like you're too close to it. What you need is objectivity."

"Is that what the dreams are telling me?"

"Partly. In your first dream, you find yourself in an underground circular enclosure with paths leading in and out from all directions. Right?"

"Exactly."

"And no matter what passageway you take, you always end up back in the enclosure."

"Yeah, until I'm so exhausted, I have to sit myself down."

"In its center."

"Is that what you're getting at? That I'm running around in circles like a fool."

"Could be," she said. "But in my books, your nobody's fool."

"Now, who's deflecting the obvious?" I volleyed back. We broke into light laughter like a pair of teenage lovers fighting off the awkwardness of their first date.

"But back to your first dream," she finally interjected, bringing us back to why I was there. "You said that you heard footsteps once you sat down in the enclosure. And that a man dressed in a white medical gown carrying a scalpel appeared."

"Yes. What do you make of that?"

"Did you know the man?

"Not that I can remember. But he had a certain familiarity to him."

"Well, it could have two meanings, but I want to stress that this is merely a hypothesis."

"Fine with me. Whatever helps untangle this mess."

"Well, Carl Jung, a contemporary of Sigmund Freud, would argue that the man in the medical garb is you, or more precisely, an archetype of yourself. Your shadow self."

"So, what you're saying is that I'm going nuts and plan to off myself?"

"No. Nothing like that. But I worry that in your line of work, you're always putting yourself in harm's way. And that there may be an underlying suicidal element at play."

"Great. Tell me something I don't know," I said jokingly.

"Trying to make light of something this important isn't good, James," throwing me a concerned look with her penetrating eyes.

"I know, doc. Can't help myself."

"Sorry, James, I didn't mean to be so harsh."

"It's all good. But what were you saying about this looney tune inside my head."

"Well, your subconscious is trying to help you cut through the entanglement you now find yourself in."

"I see. Is it a thing, or could it be a person?"

"Why? Does he remind you of someone?"

"He does. But I hadn't met him yet. I ran into him a day later when he caressed my kidneys with a sharp blade."

"That's interesting."

"Like how?" I asked, puzzled.

"Perhaps you had a vision."

"Then I am nuts. And this is your way of breaking it easy to me."

"James, many talented people have visions. You should respect and treat them as rare gifts."

"I'm all good with that if that helps me crack this case."

"Well, let's move on to your other two dreams," she said, frustrated with my evasive attitude.

"Sure. But I'll probably need those magic pills once you're done with me."

"We'll see, James. We'll see."

48

ZERO PEERED LONG and hard into the full-length mirror, admiring his work. He had applied the makeup like an expert, having spread a pancake of white foundation evenly across his face, then added a hint of red blush to accent his angular cheekbones. He used black eyeliner and mascara to bring out the glacial blue in his eyes and the ruby red lipstick—one of his favorites, that struck the right balance, accenting his thin but well-proportioned lips. The lipstick also played well with the strawberry-blonde wig and the long flowing black silk gown he wore over his sexy black lingerie. But what he adored most about his outfit were his red stiletto high heels. He loved the way it made his hips move.

It had taken him well over an hour to prepare his look. Glancing down at the time on his phone, he saw it was already nine-thirty. He'd already been there for over an hour and a half. Good thing he had booked the entire night.

Exiting his room, he maneuvered his way again through the dimly lit corridors, searching for his target, but there was no sign of him. No big deal. He knew the target would show. He had it from a reliable source, the same source that told him about Miguel's departure to Montreal.

A well-toned muscular man in his late twenties eyed Zero as she made her way down the hall. He'd been sitting alone for a good hour on one of the benches scattered throughout the place but still hadn't connected. A handful of suiters had approached him, but he brushed them off.

He had a specific type in mind, and the strawberry-blond making her way toward him was it—having become immediately aroused.

Her body movements and outfit were mesmerizing. He tried to play it cool, which was difficult, given she was coming right at him.

Without saying a word, she sat beside him and crossed her legs. He wasn't quite sure what to do next. He had been to the place only once before and had yet to learn the proper etiquette. All he wanted to do was jump her.

But the blonde made the first move, lightly placing her left hand on his knee, then turning and asking in an alluring feminine voice, "Do you have a room?"

"Yes," he blurted out.

"Show me."

49

MY SESSION WITH DR. ADAMS lasted past the allotted hour. She felt it necessary that we work through the issues before I left. Her observations and interpretations woke me up to possibilities I may have overlooked.

She'd been right about getting too close to the case. My emotions, which I usually kept well-guarded, had leaked out—the way oil does when the gasket blows on a car's oil pan. The usual solution was to drain the oil, replace the gasket, and crank the engine again. Hopefully, the problem was solved the first time around. If not, it could be days before the real issues reveal themselves. But as humans, with all our emotional and psychological baggage, that could mean years. But as it turns out, I was one of the luckier souls.

It may have had something to do with my breeding and desire to push the limits, but I had the right person to help navigate the maze. But even so, I left her office with even more questions than when I arrived.

Piña had no idea why James wanted to drive her to the train station. She had already called a cab. But he was insistent and said he had something to show her. She was on edge with this latest development, especially after seeing Lieutenant Ant the day before. The Lieutenant had asked her back to help identify a suspect who may have kidnapped her.

But once she got there and made a positive ID, the Lieutenant began asking more pointed questions about her whereabouts the day Sam disappeared.

As she had before, she told him she was home, and there was no one to back her alibi. This seemed to satisfy him, and he apologized for asking, saying it was just a routine follow-up.

The knock on the door jarred her from her thoughts. She went to open it. It was James.

"Well, hello, stranger," she said, offering her bravest smile. "You could have stayed the night if you were eager to see me again."

"I thought it would be better if we didn't. Besides, I had an errand to run."

"Oh. What kind of errand?"

"The kind that takes about ten hours."

"Whatever are you going on about, James?" It wasn't her voice but her eyes that told me she had a pretty good idea where I was going with this.

"After our talk at the café yesterday, I headed to Chicago."

"Why would you do that? And why wouldn't you have offered me a ride?" she demanded in protest, her voice also registering a hint of anger.

"Because it was something I had to do alone. I had to be sure."

"Sure, of what?" I could now spot the fear and confusion creeping into her eyes. I pulled out the small plastic bag sealed with a police sticker. Inside were the stolen diamonds from the Antwerp heist—giving off their eerie blue and green glow.

"Oh my god, James. You found them." She tried her hardest to sound excited at the sight of the gems, but it came out flat.

"You've never seen these before?" I asked.

"Never set eyes on them until now. Why are you like this? I'm getting this feeling that I'm now a suspect."

"It's funny how things work."

"How's that?"

"Well, I've been having these crazy dreams. It started about the time I met you."

"Really? What dreams?"

"There were three in total. I thought I was losing my mind until I got some help."

"Did it work?" she asked, with a hint of sarcasm and frustration.

"It did. She got me on the right path and—"

"She?"

"Yeah. The doc was of the female persuasion."

"And you didn't think of coming to me for help?"

"I didn't know you were an expert on basket cases until recently."

"What is that supposed to mean?" she asked, annoyed by my assertion.

"First, let me tell you about the dreams. Maybe you'll be able to interpret them on the first go."

"If you must," she said, moving herself to the edge of the bed, sitting and crossing her legs. I had a moment of vertigo. I wanted everything I knew about her now to just disappear. For everything to go back to the way they were.

"I had three dreams," I finally said, moving closer. "In the first one, I found myself stuck in this underground cavern filled with passages but with no way out. On the wall in front of me were these strange pictures, more like glyphs, which I later discovered were Mayan. Supposedly they referenced the end of the world, which according to some experts, would happen in 2012. But they got it wrong. We're still here—for how long, that's another question," I said, offering a dampened smile with my last point.

"I'm well versed with the Mayan Calendar and Mayan culture. It was part of my doctorate thesis, which I assume you know by now."

"I thought that might be the case, so imagine my surprise when I found out you had done extensive research on the subject."

"You could have just asked."

"At the time, I wanted to believe you had nothing to do with these," I said, glancing down at the bag of gems I was still holding. Her eyes also moved to the bag.

"You can't possibly think I had something to do with the theft?"

"Let me finish, and everything should become crystal clear. Anyway, in my second dream, the glyphs on the wall start glowing this strange yellow, and then four out of the twenty-one jump out from the wall, surrounding me."

"James, what are you—"

"Wait, let me finish. It gets even crazier from there. The glyphs morphed. And you'd never believe into what?"

"You know my train leaves in half an hour," she said, anxiously looking at her watch, wanting to change the subject badly. "You can finish your tale in the car."

"We've got plenty of time. In the worst case, I'll call in a favor from Ant and have them hold the train."

"He can do that?" she asked, naively impressed.

"Sure, he's well connected." I lied. "Anyways," wanting to return to my story, "the damn things turned into orangutans."

"What?"

"Yeah, I know. Strange, isn't it? I had to ask myself. Why orangutans and not foxes? After all, my nemesis during this entire case has been the Fox."

"That's very true," she said, intrigued by my interpretations. "So, why orangutans?"

"As far as I can figure, this whole thing started with Sam's disappearance. That's where I should have been looking, but I got sidetracked. I took Sam's disappearance as a minor element in this whole thing. And yet, she was the key."

"The key? How is that possible? She's still missing." She knew that was no longer true. It was all over her face. But she still wanted to put on a good show.

"Oh, didn't I mention that part."

"Mention what part?"

"We found Sam."

"What? Is she OK? I need to go to her at once," she said, sounding anxious and getting up abruptly, trying to move past me. I cut in front of her, grabbing her shoulders, barring her way.

"Let me go, James. You have no right."

"Perhaps, but Lieutenant Ant and Motor City's finest do."

"What are you talking about? On what grounds?"

"We found where you stashed Sam, along with the gems. At some point, I wondered why you weren't so concerned with finding her. But, like I said earlier, my judgment was clouded. I got too close to you and the case. That's what the third dream was trying to tell me. You were in it."

"How so?"

"Well, you turned into a fox and totally controlled the orangutans. You commanded them through the four passageways, each representing a direction: north, south, east, and west."

"Meaning what?"

"A case of misdirection."

"Oh, James, you don't believe that," she said, moving in tight, her breasts pressing hard against my chest, her lips only inches from mine. "Let's go away together. Just you and I."

"Where to? My passport's expired."

"Wherever you want. South America would be great at this time of year," she offered, adding a playful conspiratorial smile. "We can sell the gems once there and never have to worry about money again. We could get a hut along the sandy beaches, drinking margaritas all day."

"I'm more of a bourbon man myself. And it all sounds swell, except for one thing?"

"What's that?"

"I couldn't live with the compromise. It's just not how I'm built. Sure, it'd be fun at first, but the guilt would eat away at me over time."

"I understand," she said, moving back. "But if you change your mind..."

"Not going to happen. I can't look past everything that's happened. You're a killer and a liar."

"How dare you," slapping me hard across the face. It stung. I figured the right side of my face was now glowing a cherry red. I pawed my face to release some of its sting, but it didn't help. She had moved back several more feet and was now standing beside her language, resting on her bed. I felt like a slug that had just crawled out from under a rock—the way she was falling apart before me, but I pushed on. I wanted the truth.

"Fox made the same mistake when he sent Stonewall to my office, trying to buy me off with cash. I would never have taken the case if it wasn't for that. Runaway orangutans are just not my cup of tea."

"And what is your thing, James? Damsels in distress?"

"Sure, when the occasion presents itself," I said, allowing a beat of silence to fall between us. Then asked, "Why'd you do it? Why kill Abner? For the gems?"

"You'd never understand, James."

"Try me."

She gave me a long inquisitive stare, then turned and sat on the bed beside her language. It was hard to figure out what was going on inside her head. Finally, she seemed to come to a decision—wanting to offer me another version of her truth. It was better than nothing.

"I was worried about Sam and how he'd acted since Ombak's arrival. So that night, I returned to the Zoo to check in on them,"

"What time was that?"

"Around ten."

"Then what?"

"After checking in on them, I did some paperwork."

"What time was that?"

"Around one in the morning. Then around three, I checked in on Sam again before heading home. As I got close to her habitat, I heard this ruckus. Sam had cornered Abner, who looked terrified. He was also holding the pink pig."

"And what did you do?"

"I talked Sam down, allowing Abner to escape."

"With the gems?"

"I had no idea they existed or were stashed inside the pig."

"So, what'd you do next?"

"I went home. There was nothing else I could do. I planned to report what I saw to the Zoo authorities in the morning."

"But you didn't. And you left out this important piece of information."

"Yes. When I woke the next morning, I still felt shaken by the previous night's events. I intended to tell the Zoo about the incident, but when I got there, Sam was missing. I became so upset and confused that I forgot to mention what had happened the night before. And when I remembered, I was afraid I'd become a suspect if I said anything."

"So, you lied?"

"Yes, but you must believe me now, James. I'm now telling you the truth."

"I want to. I do. But there are just too many loose ends to your story."

"Such as?"

"You did a good job covering your tracks, but there's always a crack in any plan if you look close enough."

"And I'm assuming you found these cracks."

"It took a bit of doing. But yeah. I did. Take your alibi, for example, about where you were when Sam disappeared. You say you went home, but a street camera a few blocks from the Zoo caught you heading east toward the Zoo at around five in the morning."

"So what? It proves nothing," she fired back, hoping her anger would alter the facts.

"No, not in itself, but it's one of the cracks I'm talking about."

"I assume there are others?"

"Sure. Take the barn where we found Sam stashed in, for instance."

"Oh, yes. I was going to ask you about that," she said, sounding concerned and wanting to deflect where this was all going. "That's where you finally found Sam and the gems."

"Sure. But you already knew where Sam was. You'd been caring for her since the morning of her disappearance."

"That's absurd."

"Is it? I had Ant do an extensive background check on you, including any properties you may have owned."

"How dare you?"

Ignoring her outburst of indignation, I pushed on. "It turns out that you inherited this place from your grandmother on your father's side. You initially told me you were from Ecuador, which is true regarding being born and raised there. But you failed to mention that your father was an American citizen and had moved to Ecuador after meeting your mother at a conference here in Chicago."

"What of it? My personal life is none of your concern."

"And here you were, moments earlier, suggesting we move to Shangri-La and live happily ever after."

"That's before I realized what an asshole you really are. Besides, everything you've said up till now is all circumstantial. It'll never hold up in court."

"Well, look at you, all versed in criminal law."

"That's the problem with men like you. You take women as fools. You figure you can just bark some command, and we'll fall into place."

"Men like me. Perhaps that was true at one time, but I've changed." I couldn't believe I had just said that. She was good. She was steering the conversation away from the pertinent matter, making everything personal. We sounded like an old married couple. I needed to get back control of the interrogation.

"It's more than just circumstantial. You had motive, means and opportunity."

"Oh yeah. And what was my motive?"

"That was the hard part. I didn't figure you into the mix the first time around. Why would I? You seemed so close to your orangutans. I saw the way you and Ombak connected. And why would you wish any harm to Sam? Plus, there was the gem I found in the cage. And then Abner's rotting corpse and the pink pig— well, you created the perfect red herring."

She said nothing to that. She had turned her head and was staring at the wall behind her. I pushed on.

"Part of what you say is true. You caught Abner stealing the pig and stopped Sam from ripping him to shreds. But when you realized you were being double-crossed by the Fox, you decided to take matters into your own hands. Sure, his lawyer talked to you about Ombak. But you left a lot out."

"Like what?" she asked flatly, pretending to be bored by my summation and still staring hard at the wall.

"You were in this from the start. You knew the virus was being unleashed. You knew its implications. That it would sterilize a quarter of the world population."

"Our species must end," she said, anger and conviction now in her voice as she turned back to face me. "Everything we touch turns to poison. The orangutan population, including hundreds of other species, is on the verge of extinction. Human greed is decimating them. I could no longer stand by and watch that happen. Miguel offered me a chance to make things right."

"But when you realized that Miguel was doing his thing, not for some ideal but for purely opportunistic reasons, you got angry and fought back."

"Yes. I knew something was wrong when I caught Abner trying to steal the gems. I let him go but followed him to his place.

The guy lived like a pig, which is ironic since I was there to retrieve the pink pig from him. I knocked on his door, telling him I was there to ensure he was OK. He let me in, and I asked what he had to do with the Fox. He said he didn't know anyone named Miguel or the Fox, only that someone in a suit had approached him to steal the pig, and he'd be well compensated.

Initially, he had no idea what was inside. When he finally figured it out, he expected a bigger payday. I pleaded with him to give me the diamonds, but he said no. He then attacked me. Tried to rape me. So, I shot him. It was self-defense. You gotta believe me."

"Why not report it to the police?"

"You've got to be kidding. If I did that, and even if I got off with mitigating circumstances, I'd lose my job at the Zoo and be deported."

"I thought you didn't like the States."

"I don't. But I can't leave Sam and Ombak. Who would care for them?"

"But why sneak Sam out and hide him?"

"I figured that once they discovered Abner's body, suspicion would fall on the employees at the Zoo. So, by moving Sam to another location, I created a rouse or red herring, as you called it, making it look like Abner's murder had something to do with Sam's disappearance. And it worked till you stuck your nose in."

"Your rouse even fooled the Fox. I'm sure he had his suspicions at first. That's why he kidnapped you. Not only to play me but also to get a read on you. But you're good. He bought into the idea that the gems were with Sam. Which was true."

"So, now what, James?"

"Now I have to bring you in."

"I don't think so."

And before I knew it, she had a small caliber revolver pointed at my gut. I assumed she'd retrieved it from its hiding place under her language.

"Is that the gun you used to kill Abner?"

"What if it is?"

"Not too smart holding on to it. As you said, all I had to go on was circumstantial evidence. But the gun's a game-changer."

"Well, I'll be long gone before any of that matters."

"So, what are you going to do? Kill me in cold blood?"

"I'd never do that, James. Believe it or not, I've grown very fond of you."

"So have I. That's why it's so hard to see this happen."

"See what happen?" she asked, genuinely surprised by my response.

And on cue, Ant and two uniforms crashed through the door, their guns drawn and pointed squarely at Piña.

"Drop the gun, Miss Cornell!" Ant demanded. "It's over."

THE
RECKONING

50

I WATCHED AS ANT cuffed Piña and led her out of the room. Not another word was exchanged between us. There was nothing left to say. Perhaps, after Ant booked her, I'd visit her. But for now, I felt like crawling into a hole—a bottle of bourbon and a carton of smokes in hand and disappearing for a long while. But I knew that couldn't happen. Even though I'd solved the problem of the missing orangutan, the Fox was still on the loose. And Piña's arrest hadn't gotten me any closer to him.

Before closing the door, I looked back, scanning the room one last time. I could still picture those last few minutes with Piña—her pointing the gun at me. I had felt nothing—as though it wouldn't have mattered if she'd pulled the trigger. Dr. Adams may have been right about my suicidal tendencies. I gave my head a hard shake—hoping somehow it would erase that last thought, then shut the door behind me.

Back at the 3rd, Ant received the surveillance footage of the group I had spotted at the hotel in Montreal, including the older gentleman that had accompanied Miguel. The techs had extracted mug shots of each suspect. Ant fed the photos to all the relevant federal agencies in the country and worldwide for identification. Once identified, he told the agencies to keep a low profile while keeping the suspects under surveillance—not to spook them, hoping they would lead us to the vaccine—if one existed.

Unfortunately, I wasn't particularly good with nuances. I preferred a direct and brute-force approach. Also, I figured, if left to the powers to be, there'd be so much double-talk and diplomatic wrangling that any action would get tangled up in an international quagmire.

So far, only four of the seven suspects have been identified, with one located right here in the Motor City. The other three were in Japan, Russia, and China.

So, I devised a plan to conduct my own interrogation of the Motor City suspect, who went by the name of Charles Chapel. But it wouldn't be easy. He was some big wig associated with an international pharmaceutical conglomerate. And Ant would have the guy under surveillance. I'd need to keep out of their sightlines.

I decided to tail Chapel, starting with his workplace. He occupied an office on the thirtieth floor of a high-rise corporate building on Beverley and Fifth. I spotted him exiting the building around one—his destination, a swank restaurant that specialized in authentic French cuisine. I could never figure out why people paid exorbitant coin for such small food portions, even though the dishes looked like works of art.

I also had no way of knowing if Chapel was meeting anyone inside. I couldn't get close enough without being spotted by Ant's men or the Feds, who were scattered about. At exactly two-thirty, he exited the restaurant alone and returned to the office. At around four, he left the office building again and hailed a cab. My cab.

While Chapel was in his office, I came up with a plan. I contacted an old buddy of mine who drove a cab. I told him I had to appropriate his vehicle due to national security. He smiled, not believing me for a moment but still knowing better than to ask questions. If I needed the cab, he assumed it was important. He wanted a hundred for the cab's use.

If I got nabbed, he'd plead ignorance, and I'd have to pay for any damages. I said I was good with that, even though I had no idea how to pay for damages if something happened. Hopefully, work out a payment plan.

So, the simple part was over. The hard part was how to time Chapel's exit from the building and get him into my cab. Besides the hundred I had forked over for the cab, it cost me another Benjamin to pry favors from the cabbies at the stand in front of the office building.

My plan was simple. The next time Chapel hailed a cab, I'd be there to pick him up, right under the noses of Ant's men and the half dozen other federal agents keeping eyes on him. The plan wasn't without its faults. No plan ever was.

51

ZERO FINALLY located his target. She was sporting a short-cut, dirty blonde wig. She was also wearing a horrific paisley knee-high dress and shocking pink stockings. Her makeup was just as bad, with smudges of red lipstick running past the edges of her lips and mascara running along the sides of her eyes. She was dangerously overweight, and her plump behind was hanging over a barstool at the makeshift bar set up in one corner of the place. She was nursing a drink. Zero sat next to her and ordered a scotch straight up.

"Well, it's nice to see we share similar tastes," she said, seeing that Zero ordered the same drink. Her voice was coarse and heavy.

"That's why I sat next to you," Zero said, giving her a flirtatious smile. "You seem like a woman of taste. And I love your pink stockings."

"Why, thank you. I had them specially ordered online. What's your name? Mine's Precious."

It figured she'd have chosen such a name. Zero felt terrible for all those that held anything precious.

"I'm Angelina," Zero said, introducing himself. Is this your first time here?" he asked.

"Oh, no. I've been coming here for years. But tonight, it seems a bit slow. You?"

"My first time," adding a shy grin. "But there are a few choice hunks about."

"Oh, yes, but usually they wait till later for the sweeter-looking girls to show," she said, sizing Zero up. "You're quite the catch. I'm surprised no one's snagged you yet."

"I'm not one for these young dudes. Sure, they have a great body, but nothing much going on up here," Zero said, poking his right index finger against his head. "Plus, I like them with more meat, like yourself."

"Well, I'm flattered. Have you ever been with another girl?"

"No, I haven't. It'd be nice to see how it'd feel like."

"You gotta room?" she asked, getting excited.

"Yeah. Number nine, just down the hall. Want to come in for a drink?"

"Sure. It could be nice. But just to let you know, I like to take charge."

"No problem here," Zero said excitedly about the prospect. "Let's do this," grabbing her hand and leading her to his room.

Once inside, Zero locked the door behind him and pulled out his phone. He opened the music app and selected a tune he'd preselected for the occasion. The small portable speaker on the bed's end table came to life. He turned the volume up loud. The owners of the joint wouldn't mind. They understood some were shy about their ecstatic cries during lovemaking.

Meanwhile, Precious had already thrown off her dress, making her way towards him in what Zero could only describe as absurd and comical—like a camel who had lost its humps, its head bobbing up and down synced to its behind. When she was only several inches from Zero and about to plant him with a kiss, Zero quickly and expertly brought the six-inch blade tucked away in his garter belt to her throat.

"Ouch," Precious said, uncertain yet what had pricked her. When she finally looked down and saw the knife, she went to scream.

"I wouldn't if I were you. It'd be your last. Nod if you understand," Zero demanded. She nodded. "Good. Then we can get down to business."

Precious regained some composure, realizing that if the stranger wanted her dead, she would be already. In her mind, she wondered if this wasn't some kinky action the stranger was after. If it was, Precious wouldn't be averse to the idea. But Angelina should have given her some advance notice, that's all.

"So, what's this all about, Angelina? You like it rough?"

"Occasionally," Zero replied with a hint of a crooked smile. "But this isn't one of those times. This is, let us say, much more extreme."

"Oh?" Precious uttered, confused again.

"First, let's make ourselves comfortable on the bed, and I'll explain."

Zero released the knife's edge from her neck and did as she was told, plopping herself at the end of the bed, her back to the wall. Zero sat opposite her, placing the knife next to him as a reminder, just in case she got any ideas and ran for it.

"So, what do you want?" Precious asked as she nervously fiddled with the hem of her pink stockings.

"We have a mutual friend I'd like to discuss."

"Really. Who's that?"

"Miguel Fernandez."

Hearing the name, her eyes popped. Her breathing became heavy and shallow. She pressed herself hard against the wall, wanting to create more distance from Zero, but realized she was out of space and at a dead end. Beads of sweat accumulated across her forehead. As each bead slid down, following the contours along her eyes and down her face, the mascara and white pancake she had pasted on began to streak, creating the illusion of a sad and tormented clown.

"Who are you? What do you want?" she demanded.

"Just a bit of information. Then we can end this peacefully and go our separate ways."

"What sort of information?"

"Access to Miguel's bank accounts. You are Markos Arduino, his accountant, no?"

"Are you crazy? Do you know what he'll do when he finds out?"

"Most likely kill us both. But if I don't get what I want, I'll save him the trouble and kill you myself."

Zero brought the knife to his face, moving it back and forth, admiring it as the candlelight danced off the blade's silver surface. "If you help me, I'll help you."

"How?"

"I have a first-class plane ticket already made out in your name that leaves for a small tropical island in five hours. Miguel would never find you there."

"You can't be sure of that?"

"No, I can't, but he'll be too busy with other matters to concern himself with you."

"What about Miguel's two men downstairs. They monitor me twenty-four-seven?"

"I'll take care of that."

Markos looked long and hard into Zero's eyes, trying to weigh his options. They weren't good. Undoubtedly, he wouldn't be getting out of this room alive if he didn't give the stranger what he wanted. But then again, Miguel would surely skin him alive once he discovered he'd double-crossed him.

"First, let me see the ticket."

Zero retrieved the ticket along with the laptop from his bag. Passing the ticket to Markos, he then fired up the computer. Markos examined the ticket from back to front, ensuring it was authentic.

Satisfied, he asked, "Are you sure you want to do this? You can just let me go, and I'll tell no one about our meeting."

"I'm afraid it's a bit too late for that. Besides, I have a date with destiny and do not wish to keep her waiting."

52

I PULLED THE CAB up to the curb to let Chapel in.

"Where to?" I asked as he got into the back.

"Just drive, and I'll tell you as we go."

"Doesn't work that way," I said, cranking my neck back toward him. "Dispatch wants details on all pickups and drop-offs. It's for both our safety. Plus, it's against the law. Could get fined big time."

"There's an extra hundred in it for you. Just bend the rules this one time. No one needs to know."

"A hundred, you say. Hard to resist. So, what? I just drive."

"Yeah, and I'll tell you when and where to turn."

"Are you on the lam or something, like from your wife or some jealous lover?"

"Something like that?"

"Ok. It's your dime."

As I pulled out and headed north on Cumberland, I spotted at least five unmarked vehicles pull out one after the other in the rear-view mirror. The whole thing had the makings of a keystone comedy.

"Turn right up here on Milton, then a left on 9th Ave," Chapel commanded. I did as he said.

"Listen. If you want me to lose a tail, I can help you. I know the city. I grew up on the backstreets. And this wouldn't be my first rodeo dodging a tail. But you must tell me where we're going, so I can plan an escape."

He took his time considering my offer. He was getting more nervous by the minute, looking over his shoulder through the cab's rear window. Finally, he decided.

"Alright. If you can lose whoever's tailing us, there's another fifty on top of the hundred I promised you."

"You got it. Where to?"

"2543 Albright Rd. Know where it is?"

"Sure. Just sit back, and I'll have you there in no time. I'll leave those Feds that have been following in the dust."

"How'd you know they're Feds?"

"Who else would be so bad as tailing someone?" I said, throwing back a knowing smile.

"How do I know you're not fed?"

"You don't."

After cutting dozens of turns, jumping curbs, harrowingly missing, and sending a half dozen pedestrians back to their makers and tossing Chapel around like a discarded ragdoll in the backseat for good measure, I finally peeled around the last corner of my escape plan, skidding the car through an open door that led into a deserted warehouse.

As I came to an abrupt stop, Chapel lunged forward, his head colliding with the back of my seat. In the rear-view mirror, I caught Elvis scurrying towards the open door and shutting it. I got out, jarring open the back passenger door with my colt aimed at Chapel's head.

"Get out," I said.

He obliged with no resistance. I navigated him toward a chair that sat dead center of a thousand-square-foot warehouse that had seen better times. With a roll of gray gaffer tape in hand, Elvis spooled the tape around Chapel's body and arms, securing him to the faded yellow, straight-back wood chair.

Chapel didn't object throughout the entire process. He seemed resigned to his fate, which I found disconcerting. It'd be hard to break someone who felt they had nothing to lose.

"Who are you?" Chapel asked in a calm voice.

"The name's Cartwright. James Cartwright. I'm a private investigator."

"I see," but he didn't sound too impressed by my confession. Then turning to Elvis, he asked, "And who are you supposed to be? Wait, let me guess. You're the second coming of the King."

Elvis was all done up in his Elvis outfit, his hair gelled and slicked back with a set of gaudy-looking gold and silver bracelets hanging around his neck. He had a matinee in an hour and insisted he'd be ready for it.

"Guilty as charged," Elvis said with a wide impish grin. Chapel was one cool cucumber. There was no way I would break him by beating it out of him.

"Untie him," I said, turning to Elvis.

"What? After I just got done taping him up," but after an exasperated sigh, Elvis relented.

"You're free to go," I said. He gave me a long, hard, questioning look.

"What are you playing at, Cartwright?

"I misjudged you. I didn't do my due diligence. You have a military background, Seals if I hazard to guess, and most likely involved with black ops at some point."

"A very acute observation, Cartwright."

"But that doesn't mean you're invincible."

"No, but we both know it would take you longer to break me than I assume you have time available. Especially with Elvis there," nodding in his direction, "who's set for a grand appearance somewhere in our fair city."

"Hey, watch that mouth of yours," Elvis pushed back, "or I'll tape more than just your arms next time, dick head."

Chapel offered Elvis a knowing smile and then turned back to me, asking, "Am I really free to go?"

"Sure. But there are two things you should probably know."

"Oh yeah. What's that?"

"For one, every international organization with a multilettered acronym is tracking you and your group as we speak. It's a matter of hours before they haul your ass in. And believe me, they will have all the time in the world and highly creative ways to extract the info they want."

"And the second thing?"

"If the Feds don't get you first, Miguel will."

"What do you mean?" He had become outwardly nervous at the mention of Miguel's name. The guy had a way of doing that. It was the first crack to appear in his Chapel's self-assured armor.

"Do you think Miguel would let the seven of you control the outcome of such an elaborate scheme?"

"What scheme? I've no idea what you're talking about."

"The virus. I'm unsure of the how or why, but my gut tells me that Miguel and your group are behind it."

He gave my last words some strong consideration and, figuring he had nothing to lose and wanting to exercise his ego, said, "Miguel had nothing to do with its inception. We brought him in after the fact. We required his connection and resources."

"Sure, that's what he had you believing. I haven't known him that long, but from what I've seen so far, in how he works, the guy's an egomaniac, not unlike yourself and the others. There's no way he'd let you run roughshod on him."

"You may have a point there, Cartwright."

"I know I do. Your team's already planning an exit strategy for the creep."

"How could you possibly know that?" he asked, genuinely surprised by my inside knowledge.

"So, the information my informant gave me is true?"

"Quite true," he acknowledged, followed by a deep sigh. "And I don't mind sharing other details since they won't affect the group's plans. But I am quite impressed by your insights. We could use a person of your talents in our organization."

"Can't do. I work solo. That way, I can track who's trying to stab me in the back."

Ignoring my barb, he countered, "You can't possibly believe that Miguel has the resources to dictate the outcome of the mission?" His voice hinted at a growing doubt. The armor was unraveling.

"Before I answer that, let me ask you. How'd you get hold of the virus?" He gave me another long and questioning stare. But I could tell from his angst expression I'd hit pay dirt.

"Are you or your friend wired?" he asked, looking from me to Elvis and back again.

"No. But we could do a quick strip if you want and if you're into that sort of thing."

"That won't be necessary. I'll take you at your word. As for the answer to your question, which you've already surmised, Miguel supplied us with it."

"He wouldn't have gotten it from an old, short, scrawny guy that walks with a limp," I asked.

"Yes," he said, his face turning paler and the timbre of his voice growing weaker. "What exactly are you trying to get at with these questions?"

"I assume there's a vaccine kicking around. There's no way you'd release the virus without assuring your kind would survive."

"Correct. And we've inoculated ourselves."

"And did you, by any chance, experience similar symptoms to the virus that's going around?"

"Why? We were told by the doctor that we would. It was part of the special vaccine's side effects that he gave us. What are you—" but Chapel cut himself short. The full implication of what I had been driving at hit him like a meteor slamming into the Gobi Desert. "It can't be."

"I wasn't sure myself till now," I said. "But based on what you've told me, the odds are your group never received the vaccine but the virus itself. Which can mean only one thing?"

"What's that?" Elvis asked, cutting in, intrigued and anxious for my answer.

"That there never was a vaccine, or if there is one, Miguel and his doctor friend still possess it."

"Jesus Christ. What are we supposed to do now?" Elvis blurted out.

Turning to him, I said, "You, nothing. You've stuck your neck out far enough. Come on, I'll drop you off at your gig."

"What about him?" Elvis asked, pointing to Chapel.

"Leave him. He'll find his way back."

We turned and made our way to the caddy. As we were about to get in, Chapel shouted, "Wait!"

I gave Elvis a conspiratorial grin and turned my attention back to Chapel.

"What is it, Chapel?"

"I have something to offer. I know where you can find that doctor."

"I'm all ears."

"Before I do, you must promise to go to the address I gave you when you picked me up."

"The 2543 Albright address?"

"Yeah, that's the one."

"Why's that?"

"My daughter lives there. I need you to tell her to leave the city. And after I tell you what I'm about to tell you, my life won't be worth a damn. And neither will hers."

"I promise. If what you're about to tell me is on the level."

"It is. And the virus isn't what you think it is."

53

WHAT DO YOU MEAN my accounts were compromised?" Miguel screamed. "How is that possible?"

"We figure someone's hacked them," said the tall, lanky young man who had brought him the bad news.

"But by who? How? Where's that poor excuse for a human being at?"

"You mean your accountant?"

"Yes. That sloth."

"We haven't been able to locate him, sir."

"But how do you know there's a problem with the accounts?"

"Someone phoned and told us so."

"What? This sounds more preposterous by the minute. Bring me my laptop. I want to check for myself."

The messenger did as he was told, exiting the room and returning minutes later with the requested item. Miguel grabbed it, placing it on the office desk before him. It took several minutes for the computer to come online and for Miguel to feed the information his offshore bank account required to log in. Miguel had over fifty-million worth of ill-gained American dollars stashed in there, most of it gained during the Dirty Wars.

The expression on his face said it all but expressed his newly found devastation by picking up the gun next to his laptop and firing one clean shot through the messenger's forehead. The messenger's face expressed disbelief, his eyes rolling back into his head, hoping to capture and stop the bullet's trajectory. But instead fell back with a thump, like a sack of potatoes, onto the floor.

"Andreas," Miguel shouted at the top of his lungs. A newly minted rendition of the one that had just fallen rushed in.

"Yes, Mr. Fern—" stopping short of tripping over his comrade.

"Get the car ready."

"Yes, sir."

"And find out where that pig of an accountant has disappeared to?"

"Yes, Mr. Fernandez."

Zero was back at his spot outside Miguel's hideout in Grosse Pointe. Ten minutes earlier, he had made an anonymous phone call to the residence, informing the person on the other end about Miguel's now depleted bank account. He felt somewhat bad for relaying this critical information to the young man who answered the phone. Knowing Miguel, he figured he'd sealed the young man's fate.

Sure enough, ten minutes later, he heard the gunshot echo from somewhere near the front of the house. Another five minutes passed before he saw Miguel and two of his minions run out the front door and speed off in the black BMW SUV. So far, everything was going to plan. Miguel was starting to fall apart.

He heard the twig snap behind him but was too late to react.

"Don't move," a familiar voice demanded. Zero weighed his options, which weren't good, especially if the voice had a gun pointed at his back. So, he did as he was told.

"Lift your hands so I can see them." Cartwright ordered, "and turn around real slow like."

"We meet again, my friend," Zero said, turning and revealing a dumb grin plastered across his face.

"I'm not your friend. And I don't know you."

"That may be so, but the last time we met, we had a common goal and enemy."

"I remember. And even though we may share a common enemy, as you say, I doubt our goals are mutually exclusive."

"Agreed," Zero said, still holding on to his grin. Then asked, "May I get up?"

"Not yet. First, empty your pockets and place their contents before you." Cartwright watched him withdraw a brown leather wallet, some cash and coins, a set of keys and a burner phone.

"Ok, now the knife?"

"What knife?" he asked, his grin widening even further like some mad joker from a Batman comic.

"The one you've got hidden in your back."

"Oh, that knife." Zero reached to extract the knife.

"Real slow, now," Cartwright added, giving his colt a nudge in Zero's direction to back up his point.

"Now drop it in front of you, stand up as if you've just taken a crap and then move back ten steps."

"Such imagery, Mr. Cartwright."

Once Zero was safely out of reach from his knife, Cartwright moved in, pushing it behind him with his foot.

"Satisfied?" Zero asked.

"I will be when you've answered all of my questions to my liking."

"And then what? Turn me over to the authorities?"

"Unless you give me a good reason not to. Your info about Fox being in Montreal was solid and offered some good leads. But why give it to me? If you say, Miguel is a mutual enemy, why not just kill him?"

"Because, like you, I'm also interested in saving lives."

"The virus?"

"Yes. And if I kill Miguel without first getting hold of the vaccine...."

"What are you? A cold-blooded killer with a moral code?"

"We share a commonality," The grin was gone. His expression serious. "You may not be a killer-for-hire like myself, but many bodies drop dead wherever you go."

Cartwright figured he had a point there. "But why the sudden concern about what happens to others?"

"Because I detest the loss of innocent lives. The ones I target have brought their fate by their actions. I've seen much too much senseless death in my life, especially in my youth during the junta."

"That's where you know Miguel from?"

"Yes. I was recruited as a teenager to serve in the Death Squads."

"But why go after him now? I'm sure you've had plenty of opportunities throughout the years?"

"Because now, it's part of my preordained destiny, one I must fulfill."

Cartwright thought the guy was probably off his rocker, but he didn't have all day to work around that. He had to find the vaccine—if one even existed. Chapel revealed that the man with Miguel in Montreal was Emanuel Degas, the scientist behind the virus. He also told Cartwright he was held up at Miguel's.

"I assume you have some sort of plan to get inside."

"I do," he said, the grin reappearing.

"Ok. Lead the way."

"I'll need my blade back just in case," eyeing the knife Cartwright had kicked behind him.

Cartwright gave Zero a long hard look, trying to gauge how far he could trust him but couldn't get a read. Cartwright had no choice but to relent.

"One false move, and I'll fill you with lead."

"So American. But yes, I understand."

"And one last thing."

"Yeah?"

"No killing unless absolutely necessary."

"As I said, we have a lot in common."

54

I FOLLOWED THE ONE who called himself Zero down the steep incline towards Miguel's place. Only two guards were on duty since the other two had rushed off with Miguel twenty minutes earlier. I wasn't sure what that was about, but the Fox seemed quite upset. I asked Zero if he knew why.

"Let's just say he's out-of-pocket change," he answered cryptically, with that damn grin of his flashing across his face once again.

"You wouldn't have had something to do with that?"

"I had a nice long talk with his accountant the other night, and we came to an understanding."

"I bet."

We were now at the perimeter of the house. The iron-wrought six-foot fence that encircled the property was still in our way.

"Any idea how to get in?" I asked.

"Just follow me."

We made our way carefully around to the back, keeping an eye out for the guards. They had other things on their mind and were not following their usual routines. Having reached our destination, Zero crouched down, grabbing two fence rails.

Giving them a quick pull, they gave way. He repeated the process for the two rails on either side. A six-foot square opening was now looking back at us. His magic trick impressed me. He explained that he had replaced the original rails with wood copies.

"You never cease to amaze me. Gotta keep a real close eye on you."

"If that's your way of complimenting me, then I accept. Now, let's go."

"Wait!" I whispered, tapping him on the shoulder, having spotted a guard. The guard had taken his duties seriously again. Even though we were a couple hundred yards away, I didn't want to chance it. We quickly pulled back out of sight into the shrubs and waited. I was hoping for the guard's sake he wouldn't spot us, or it could get messy, especially now that the stranger had his knife back. But luck was on our side. The guard quickly moved out of sight toward the other side of the house.

"Ok. Now let's move," I said.

We made a run for it across the well-manicured lawn. The grass, still soggy from last night's rainfall, triggered a squish-squash sound below our feet. I had to focus on not slipping since the soles of my shoes were worn thin. I meant to replace them but had grown fond of them, so I always delayed the inevitable.

Finally, we made it to the backdoor but found it locked. Zero gave me a questioning look. I dug into my pant pocket and pulled out a set of lock pics. I went to work, and we were in, in under a minute.

We found ourselves in a spacious, well-equipped kitchen with bleach-white walls, mahogany-stained cupboards with glass inserts and a beautifully inlaid Portuguese Azulejo tiled floor. We moved past the kitchen island that still held remnants of a half-eaten meal, making our way to a long hallway leading to three rooms on either side of us and a foyer at the front of the house.

The first two rooms turned out to be makeshift bedrooms, with a couple of cots and dressers, probably to host Miguel's goons. The third room we entered gave me cause for pause.

A young man, I'd say in his late twenties, was lying on the floor in front of a large office desk. I figured we were in Miguel's office. I went to the body to check for a pulse. Nothing. His face was caked with drying blood that looked like a Rorschach inkblot test without the faintest notion of what I was supposed to see. But one thing was clear—a bullet had neatly burrowed its way through his forehead.

"Any idea what happened here," I asked, returning my attention to Zero.

"Let's just say he was the messenger."

"Messenger for what?"

"That loss of income I was telling you about earlier."

Ignoring his penchant for riddles, I said, "ok, let's check out the rest of the house before Miguel gets back."

We exited the room and headed to the spiral staircase off the foyer. But first, I glanced through one of the glass panes that made up a third of the solid oak door that fronted the drive. The two guards were chatting it up again, and no sign of Fox.

Reaching the top of the staircase, we were again met with a hallway leading to a series of doors, except this time, we hit pay-dirt on our first try.

A thin, elderly man I had seen with Miguel in Montreal was seated behind a desk. His face was even paler and more haggard than I remembered, and the sockets around his eyes held a sickly red tint, like someone who'd been crying excessively. He also had a gun pointed at us.

"Who are you?" he demanded. I wasn't sure how to play this out. But I didn't need to.

"Emanuel?" Zero asked.

"Yes. And who are you?"

"My name is Alejandro Petra."

He gave Zero a long, penetrating stare, then said, "It can't be. You're dead. I heard that the Policia Federal had cornered you during a raid, and when you refused to give up, you were shot and killed."

"You must never believe everything you read in the papers, Emanuel," offering a friendly smile with his words.

"But how do I know it's you? My memory is not what it used to be. And your face, the way you look, has changed so much?"

"Ask me something that only I would know. Like the time when you, I and Miguel were on that farm. It was hot and humid, and we talked about how we would someday make Argentina great again."

"That doesn't mean anything."

"Or when I came to you in the middle of the night with a bullet wound. The resistance had ambushed me, and you patched me up. The scar's still there." Zero pulled up his shirt, revealing a long-jagged scar on his lower right side.

"It is you. Oh my god, it is so great to see you again after all this time. Look at me now, how I've grown old and weak, nothing like the young man I was back then. And yes, you're right. We did believe anything was possible then, and no one could stop us."

"Yes, those were special times," Zero replied in a nostalgic tone.

"But why have you come here without Miguel's knowledge, sneaking around like a common thief? And who is this stranger you've brought with you?" he demanded, suddenly changing his tone and focusing his gun directly on me.

My concern was not so much that he was pointing the gun at me but how badly his hands were shaking, increasing the possibility that it could go off at any minute by accident.

"If you don't mind pointing that gun elsewhere," I said, "we can answer all of your questions to your satisfaction."

"I still didn't get an answer," he threw back, ignoring my compromise.

"My name's James Cartwright. I'm a private investigator," I answered, relenting to his demand.

"Good. That's a start, but it still doesn't answer the second part of my question. Why are you here?" For an aging artifact, the old geezer still had plenty of spunk.

"Hopefully, to talk some common sense into you."

"Oh, I see now. You're looking for the vaccine. I'm sorry to disappoint you, but there isn't one. I created this virus to fulfill my lifelong dream, to rid this planet of the real virus that inhabits it."

"Which is?"

"Us, we *Homo sapiens*," he responded with an expansive circular gesture of his arm, including Zero and me as part of his equation.

I instinctively ducked as I watched his gun ride along the arc of his arm. But I also decided to make my move. I took two quick strides toward him, grabbing his arm on the downswing and jamming the side of my palm against his wrist, causing the gun to fall to the floor.

He gave out a sharp cry. It must have hurt since my palm was aching from the maneuver. But within seconds, Emanuel was back to his confrontational self.

"So, what now? You have my gun. It makes no difference. And I'm not afraid to die."

"Emanuel, listen, I've come here to tell you something," Zero cut in, his voice soft and pleading. This guy was growing on me. The dichotomy and complexity of his character intrigued me.

"What could you possibly have to tell me, especially after this betrayal," pointing his index finger at me as if I were the root of all his problems.

"It's about your son, Arturos." Emanuel's face turned several shades paler at the mention of his son's name, if that was even possible. Hollywood would have easily cast him as Bela Lugosi's double in Count Dracula.

"What about my son?"

"I know you created the virus to avenge your son's death. You blame the Americans for their intervention into our affairs that eventually led to the death of your son."

"Yes. If it hadn't been for them," giving me a barbed glare and look of accusation that made my skin cold, "my son would still be alive today."

"And in part, my friend, you are correct," Zero said. "Many are to blame for the misfortunes that befell our beloved country during those dark times. But what if I were to tell you that wasn't the reason he died? His death was executed by those you loved and trusted?"

"What are you saying?" getting up and moving toward Zero. He was now shaking uncontrollably.

"Perhaps you should stay seated."

"No. Just tell me."

Zero stared fondly at his old friend. I'd swear there were tears in his eyes. "It was me, Emanuel. I executed your son."

"What? No, it can't be. Why? Why would you have done such a thing?"

"Here, sit down," Zero said, taking hold of Emanuel's shoulders. Emanuel's shaking intensified, his legs ready to fold under him.

"No. Don't touch me," he shouted, flinging his arms up to disengage from Zero's grasp, causing himself to be propelled back. I moved in, breaking his fall and catching him by the shoulders. I then eased him back into the chair.

Zero waited till he thought Emanuel had calmed down enough, then said, "Emanuel, you must hear me out. After that, you can decide who or what to believe."

"Why Alejandro? Why would you have done such a thing?"

"I was ordered too."

"By whom?"

"By Miguel."

The shock of this revelation put Emanuel into a spasm, his shaking now so violent it pushed the chair he was sitting in several inches back. Again, Zero waited patiently until he calmed down.

"Never," Emanuel finally managed to say. "Miguel would never order such a thing. And why? What would have been his reasons?"

"Your son was considered a delinquent and a disgrace to the party."

"What are you saying?"

"Arturos was a Marxist, Emanuel. But you knew that?"

"Yes, I did. He told me a few nights before he disappeared. I was so angry. We never had a chance to discuss it further." Emanuel's voice had softened, and the anger he had shown earlier seemed to drain from his body. "I did everything I could to convince him to be discreet, but it was useless. I explained that his life was in danger if anyone should find out. And now you're telling me it was you and Miguel behind his death…."

"I'm so sorry to be the one to tell you this—"

"So, why do so after all these years?"

"To show you what kind of person Miguel is. You cannot trust him. He cares only for himself and nothing about ideals. He's only in it for power and money. Even back then."

"And now you think your confession will soften me up, so I'll give you the vaccine."

"No. That you'll do it in the memory of your son. We both know he would not have wanted all this death and pain. Especially not in his name."

Zero had hit a chord with the old man. Tears flowed effortlessly. And without another word, Emanuel opened a drawer to his desk. He pulled out a sheet of paper, scribbling something onto it. Then folding it into quarters, he handed it to me and said, "Here. Give this to your scientists. They'll know what to do with it."

But as I was about to thank him, I saw the bedroom door edge open. I shouted, "Zero, behind you."

As Zero turned to face the oncoming threat, the guard, having also heard my warning, reacted. He burst through the door, his gun aimed and ready. I got three rounds off to his two. He went down fast and hard. I moved to where he had fallen, kicking his dislodged gun to the side. Returning my attention to Zero, I saw him standing next to Emanuel. One of the guard's bullets had found a home in Emanuel's chest. Zero was checking for a pulse. He shook his head, letting me know he was gone.

I could now hear the second thug making his way up the stairs, calling out to his mate. I flattened myself up against the wall next to the door and waited. As he pushed through the door, I brought my gun down hard on his wrist, causing his gun to drop to the floor. I followed that with a quick right jab to his gut and an uppercut to his face. He was out for the count.

I turned to Zero and asked, "Can you clean up the mess?"

"Why, where are you going?"

"I need an expert opinion about what Emanuel scribbled on this paper," which was now safely tucked away in the inner pocket of my suit jacket.

"How do I know you won't have your friends come crushing in to arrest me?"

"You don't. You'll have to trust me."

"Does that mean you trust me?" Zero asked, a wry smile on his face.

"Not exactly. But do either of us have a choice."

"No." Zero admitted.

"Well, then it's settled. Once you've cleaned this up, head back to the spot on the hill. Call me the moment Miguel shows."

"So, you want me to wait. Do nothing."

"That about sums it up. Until we know if what Emanual gave us is real, we'll need Miguel alive as insurance."

"Understood."

I took a minute, trying to read his long, drawn face—would he wait or kill Miguel on site, but like before, it was impossible to decipher. I jotted down the number for my burner phone and left without another word being spoken between us.

MOTOR CITY

55

PIÑA LAY PROSTATE and helpless on the concrete floor, struggling to get up but unable to do so. Her legs felt like putty. A shadow from the opposite corner had moved toward her. She couldn't make out who it was, but the gun he carried left no doubt about his intent.

She understood it was a dream but did nothing to alter her terror. She sensed the identity of the shadow—it had followed her throughout her life—from when she was a child still living in Ecuador.

A man they called *El dueño* had come for the black-headed spider monkey, a rare species close to extinction. Piña had found the monkey deep in the rainforest, injured. Over time, she carefully nursed it back to health.

But El dueño, an influential figure, who owned most properties in her town, including the one her parents rented, demanded she releases the monkey into his custody.

He said an American buyer was willing to pay top dollar for it. Piña refused. Her father intervened, claiming El dueño had no right to demand such a thing, even though he knew it meant eviction for him and his family.

El dueño swore he'd be back with the authorities, which Piña knew wasn't true since spider monkeys were a protected species. But she did not trust him, so that night, she snuck her father's rifle into bed and waited.

Sure enough, El dueño returned alone in the middle of the night.

He jarred open her bedroom window, making his way in. The monkey, which she had called Querida, meaning *dearest*, was on the bed beside her and started screeching upon hearing the intruder.

Piña pointed the gun at El dueño, who stood hidden in the shadows. She told him to get out, or she'd shoot. Ignoring her warning, he went to grab the monkey. She fired once, forcing El dueño to stumble back hard against the bedroom door.

Her father, hearing the ruckus, ran to her aid. Pulling open the door to her bedroom, El dueño fell through, landing on the kitchen floor with a loud thud—dead as the night.

Her father called the authorities, claiming El dueño snuck into her room to assault her. They knew there were plenty of holes in her story, such as what she was doing with her father's shotgun in her bed in the middle of the night. But they let it go. No one liked El dueño. Everyone, including local officials and the cops, was glad to have rid themselves of him.

It was morning, and James had promised to visit her. She wasn't sure if she wanted him to see her as she was now—frail, frightened and locked behind these cold steel bars. She found it ironic that she should be caged like the creatures she loved and tried hard to protect.

56

WE COULD HAVE WAITED and ambushed Miguel upon his return. Or gone through the proper channels and brought Ant into the loop. But I decided against both possibilities. I wasn't sure what Emanuel had scribbled onto the paper. Was it indeed the key to a vaccine? But in case it wasn't, Miguel was my last resort—once again, coming out on top.

I never doubted that Miguel was clever, intelligent, narcissistic, and mad. He also had an uncanny amount of luck that increased his odds of survival. Then again, he made his luck by insulating himself with layers of protection—from thugs who swore allegiance to him to the Chapels of this world who rigged the system or the corrupt politicians fueled by greed.

The virus was now raging out of control throughout the world. Politicians and their like were scurrying for cover. Conspiracy theorists pushed every inconceivable reason for the virus's origin—tying it to the great *reset* by the deep state or an attempt to inject microchips through vaccines to control and monitor the masses. Then some decided they were immune to the virus, spreading it exponentially,

All I knew for sure was that no one had any idea what was happening and what could happen except the guy who had scribbled the cure on a scrap of paper.

So, I decided to reach out to The Stooges. I first met them through Elvis at a comedy club, where their shtick was to impersonate The Three Stooges, a comedy and vaudeville act active from the 30s to the 70s. I know what you're thinking—how could I seriously entrust the future of humanity to three grown men who identified themselves with a past vaudeville act? As it turns out, the three shared a half dozen doctorate degrees between them.

First, there was Jimmy Salva, who role-played the character Larry from The Three Stooges. Jimmy held two Ph.D. degrees, one in microbiology and the other in advanced chemistry. But his specialty was biohacking—creating and experimenting with things like frogs that glowed red in the dark or unique implants inserted under the skin, which, when connected to a mobile device, could monitor and send critical information about one's body. In certain situations, the implant could also control and trigger neurological responses.

Next was Samson Bird, who identified with Curly from The Three Stooges. His specialty was communications. As impressed as I was with Elvis's ability to hack, Curly was the Mozart of the cyber world. There was nothing he couldn't hack. He also had extensive contacts within the Dark Web, which had come in handy when a case required a more unsavory means to achieve my goals.

And finally, there was Moe Mark. Moe was the group's frontman and researcher. He also managed their blog and newsletter promoting their brand of conspiracies. For the most part, it was backed by verifiable facts. I held the dubious honor of having several of my cases featured in it. Their blog and newsletter were appropriately named, *The Stooges: Critical Investigations into Unexplained Phenomena.*

"James," I heard Moe shout through the door, followed by a half dozen deadbolts being released. When the door finally opened, he threw me a hug. Samson and Jimmy would then join him, taking turns with the hugs. As usual, I was obliged to stand until they all completed their ritual. They once explained that the hugs weren't as benign as they first appeared. They were checking for any electronic bugs a visitor was trailing in, purposely or unwittingly.

"What brings you to our fine establishment, James?" It was Jimmy asking.

"I have something I'd like you all to look at."

I took the scrap of paper from my pocket and placed it on one of their work benches. The all crowded around to have a look.

"Looks like hieroglyphics to me," Samson offered.

"The top five lines look like some DNA, RNA sequencing," Jimmy said.

"Where'd you get it, James? And why is it important?" Moe asked.

"Supposedly, it's the cure for the virus stalking our fair city."

"No shit," Samson said.

"What do you think? Is it the real thing?' I asked.

"It's possible," Jimmy returned. But without the sequencing of the original virus, it may not be much help.

"Hold on, let me have a closer look," Samson said, moving between Moe and me, grabbing the paper and scurrying back to his bench, which held several monitors and keyboards. Now seated in front of one, he furiously began pressing keys on the keyboard.

"What's he doing?" I asked Moe, who was standing next to me as we now peered over Samson's shoulders.

"Accessing the Dark Web. First, he needs to activate his Tor browser. It's the only way to access it. Normal browsers like Firefox and Safari won't work."

"I'll take your word for it," having no idea what he was referring to.

The screen on the monitor had turned a light graduated shade of green. At the top of the screen, an image of an onion appeared with the words, *Welcome to Tor Browser. You're Now Free To Browse The Web Anonymously.*

"What's with the onion?"

"It means that from here on, I'll be using an *onion router* to navigate to the site while masking my identity as I move through the dark web. Imagine an onion with its multiple layers." Samson explained without turning back.

"The technique was developed by the U.S Navy back in the mid-90s," Moe chipped in, "not unlike the internet, which was a project originally financed by the U.S. Department of Defense back in the '60s."

"Leave it up to Uncle Sam to instigate such nefarious devices. But why not keep it to themselves?" I asked.

"They didn't understand its full potential," Moe explained. "It wasn't till the early eighties that scientists and researchers began assembling a network using a standardized system to communicate with each other through the net. But it wasn't until the early 90s that a computer scientist named Tim Berners Lee unlocked the true power of the net by creating a standardized browser called Netscape. It allowed everyone to surf the World Wide Web and turn it into the phenomena we know today."

"I'm only too glad the U.S. Post Office still exists. Never understood why people are so hurried to talk to one another. Nothing ever good comes out of it, except perhaps, misunderstanding and regret, for words spoken in the heat of the moment."

"Always the cynic, eh, James," Samson teased.

"I'd say cautious, being the operative word."

Turning back to Jimmy, I watched as he punched the sequence of letters and numbers from the sixth line of Emanuel's scrap paper that read *ecji8vo3z2lzza96* into the computer. Samson followed the sequence with a period and the word onion. Then he hit the return key. The monitor went dark briefly, followed by a bright yellow background. A purple-colored sphere surrounded by what looked like short red spikes then appeared. A rectangular white box sat just beneath the sphere.

"What the hell is that supposed to be?" I asked.

"It's what a virus looks like under a microscope," Jimmy said. "Most likely the one terrorizing the world. Nature is amazing in that something so small can cripple the all-mighty Homo sapiens."

"Amazing!" Moe blurted out in agreement.

"Sure, if you're not at the receiving end," Samson added.

"Well, let's see if we can't rectify that." Jimmy countered, punching in another thirteen-letter and number sequence into the white box on the screen. It was the seventh and final line written on Emanuel's paper. A second later, the screen exploded with an array of diagrams.

"Jesus, Mary of God," Jimmy blurted out.

"What? What is it?" I asked, with no idea of what I was looking at.

"Well, from the looks of it," Jimmy said, turning to face me with a glowing grin, "we've hit the mother lode. Whoever wrote this, they've given us the complete RNA breakdown of the virus. From what I can make out," he continued, having turned his attention back to the monitor, "not only does he show how the virus was manipulated but also the projection of cases and deaths that would accompany the virus's release."

"This doctor of yours must be one sick cookie," Moe said.

"What about the cure?" I asked Jimmy, ignoring Moe's commentary.

"Well, I'm assuming that the other sequences he's written on this paper have something to do with the cure. I'll need more time to go through everything to be sure."

"How long?"

"At least a few hours."

"OK, keep in touch. I've got somewhere else to be. You can reach me at this number," I said, pulling out the burner phone that Ant had given me.

"Look at James, getting hip to the latest tech," Samson said, joking.

"Believe me, it's only temporary," I threw back. "Once the case is over, so is this contraption."

"Come on, James, you can't keep going through life ignoring progress and not adapting to the changes. Look what happened to the dinosaurs." Moe said, ribbing me.

"Go ahead. Have a few laughs at my expense, but remember, we wouldn't be in this predicament if progress had taken it somewhat slower."

"Point taken, James, but—" Samson said.

"But nothing. Call me as soon as you have something. And not a word of this to anyone till you hear from me. Understood?"

"Understood." Moe, Samson, and Jimmy replied in unison. I then turned and rushed out, realizing I was late for an earlier appointment.

57

PIÑA WAS BEING HELD at the Detroit Detention Center on Mound Road. The Michigan Department of Corrections and the Motor City's Police Department ran the place under an interagency deal. Detainees awaiting arraignment were held there for at least seventy-two hours. I heard from Ant they had scheduled Piña's arraignment for two o'clock the next day with the 36th District Court.

I parked my caddy in one of the few available parking spots and went to the second of the two buildings that made up the DDC. The first building was used for administrative purposes, while the second was for the detainees. Ant had pulled some strings since only lawyers were allowed in before arraignments. I'd also arranged for an old buddy of mine to act as Piña's lawyer.

Piña was waiting for me, seated behind a large white laminated rectangular table. She offered a weak smile as I entered—nothing near the brilliance I was used to seeing from her. The guard who'd escorted me in pointed to the empty chair opposite Piña and told me that no physical contact was allowed.

"Hello, James," Piña said once the guard had left. Until then, she held me like a lost puppy with her eyes.

"Hi, Piña. How are they treating you?"

"OK, I guess. Though I cannot judge since I've never experienced anything like this before." Her voice hinted at a certain finality. I was concerned. After I left, I'd get Ant to put her on suicide watch.

"I've got some news about the virus."

"Really. What?"

"We may have discovered a cure."

"That's wonderful, James," but she didn't sound enthusiastic about the news. "How?"

"Let's just say that the doctor who developed it had a change of heart."

"You are very persuasive when you want to be."

"Well, it wasn't all my doing. I had help," I said with a faint smile. Getting no response, I asked, "Did Renaldo, that lawyer friend of mine, get in touch with you?"

"Yes, he did. But you mustn't have James. The court would have appointed one for me."

"You don't want to use one of theirs. It's a death sentence." I regretted my choice of words the moment I said them. "What I mean—"

"I know what you meant, James. It's OK. But I can't have you spending money…."

"That's not a problem. He owes me big for getting him out of a jam a few years back."

"So, is that what you're here to tell me? You're the knight in shining armor that's come to rescue me, even though you're why I'm here." Seeing the shock of her words register across my face, she immediately added," I'm so sorry, James, I didn't mean to—"

"No, you're right to be angry. I've got a lot of guilt about what happened between us rattling inside my head."

She reached across the table, placing her hand over mine, sending a shock of emotive energy through my body. I didn't realize till then how much I cared for her. But the event was short-lived.

"No contact," boomed an ominous voice over the loudspeakers. I felt transported into an Orwellian dystopia.

"Were you able to get hold of the zoo?" I asked as she slowly and cautiously removed her hand. I now felt an overwhelming sense of emptiness from her gesture.

"Yes. Sam and Ombak are back together and bonding well."

"That's great to hear."

"I guess you miss them a lot?" I asked stupidly.

"Very much so."

I sensed our conversation was losing ground fast and slipping into monosyllabic grunts. So, I pushed on with the second reason for my visit.

"Listen, I need to ask you something." The expression in her eyes said it all. They shifted from light to dark, as if witnessing a solar eclipse, but unlike an eclipse, they remained in darkness.

"Ask away."

"Do you remember any other details about your visit with the lawyer or Miguel?"

"Like what?"

"Something they may have said or details they may have let slip during their conversation."

"No. Not that I can recall." She paused for a beat, searching harder. "Wait a minute. Miguel took this one phone call while I was at the unit. It was just as I was being escorted back to my room."

"Yes."

"Well, I'm not sure if it means anything."

"Anything will help."

"Miguel asked whoever was on the line if the plane was ready?"

"And?" Coaxing her on.

"And there were these numbers Miguel repeated out loud as if trying to set them to memory. I think they were AF51347 or something like that. I'm sorry, but I can't be sure."

"That's OK. That may be enough to help."

"Do you really think you can get him?"

"Well, I've had him in my crosshairs twice. The first time he got away because it was beyond my control. And yesterday, when I could have nailed him, I decided not to."

"But why?"

"Because it wasn't the right time. The virus took priority. But the next time we meet, there'll be no escape. I'll make sure of it."

"I hope you're right. He's a dangerous and deceptive individual. Promise me you'll be careful."

"I promise."

She reached out, taking hold of my hand once again.

Leaving Piña, I retrieved my gun, phone, wallet, and loose change from the cardboard box the guard had stored on the shelf behind him. I noticed that I had missed a call. I didn't recognize the number but was pretty sure who it was. Only five people with the number were Ant, Sangria, Elvis, Zero and The Stooges. It couldn't be Sangria, Ant or Elvis, so it left only two possibilities—Zero or The Stooges. I redialed the number, and Moe answered on the second ring.

"James?"

"What'd you find out?"

"I'd rather not say over the phone." Moe was being his typical paranoid self.

"OK, I'll come right over," I said, frustrated that I'd have to wait another twenty minutes and a pat down for an answer. And hung up.

58

ZERO HAD PROMISED Cartwright he'd do nothing rash. He said he'd return to his spot on the hill, keep an eye out, and call when Miguel showed. But lied. He had no intention of doing what he said. He planned to confront Miguel—a heart-to-heart was in order and long overdue.

An hour after Cartwright's departure, he heard a vehicle pull up in the driveway. Zero was still in Emanuel's room, wanting to spend time with his old friend—a personal wake of sorts. He had disposed of the two guards—one still breathing but gagged and tied, into the closets of the other two bedrooms.

He had moved Emanuel to the couch, laying him out vertically, with his arms resting and crossed against his chest—his friend finally looking at peace. But Zero knew one could never be sure what awaited one after their mortal coil had been extinguished. He believed it was beyond anyone's comprehension, no matter what their religion claimed. Zero didn't fear death. He had made peace with it a long time ago. Death was, after all, part and parcel of his existence.

He took the gun from the desk, which Emanuel had used on Cartwright and him, and pocketed it into his suit jacket. He may need it if Miguel comes up with his goons. But he was betting Miguel would come alone, leaving the other two guards to search the grounds for the other two.

Sure enough, five minutes later, Miguel walked in. The expressions on Miguel's face would have been almost impossible to describe if one had asked Zero about it. They shifted from utter surprise to confusion, from astonishment to disappointment, from anger and resentment to sadness and finally, resignation.

"What have you done, Alejandro?"

"This." he said, "is your fault," pointing to Emanuel. It's the inevitable outcome of what you started many years ago."

"You fool. You have no idea what you've done. You've damned us all."

"How's that?"

"Emanuel was the only one who had the vaccine to the virus spreading everywhere."

"I know," Zero said with a widening grin.

"You know?" Then it hit Miguel. "He gave it to you?"

"In a manner of speaking. And it seems he didn't entrust you with it. He understood you better than I thought. It was his ace in the hole."

"You haven't changed a bit from the first time we met. Still the joker, eh, Alejandro. I could never get a straight answer from you, then or now."

"The trouble with you, Miguel, is you always see things in black and white. You're unable to experience or understand the subtle beauty that surrounds us. Greed and hatred are the only things that drive you."

"Perhaps, but I never fooled myself into believing I'm something I'm not. "Tell me, do you still dress up?" Miguel asked in a mocking tone.

"That is none of your concern," Zero threw back a bit too defensively.

"Yes. Perhaps you're right," Miguel said, knowing he had made his point, "but killing Emanuel. That is not right."

"It was your idiot guard that did that. He burst into the room while Emanual and I were talking. So, I reacted."

"By shooting him. No. That's not your style. Someone else was here with you. But who?" directing the question more to himself.

"It can't be. Or can it? It must have been that pest, the PI."

"Who?"

"Don't play dumb with me, Alejandro. You know very well who I mean. That bumbling detective that has an uncanny way of getting his nose into everything while leaving behind Armageddon wherever he goes."

"Look who's calling who the grim Reaper. All the blood that stains your own hands cannot even compare."

"And what about you, my dear Alejandro?"

"I know who I am and what I've done. But that's all over now. I've now chosen to leave that life."

"And do what? Raise sheep? Who's fooling who, now?"

"I don't need you to believe me, and I'm not looking for your blessings. I've come here to finish what I should have done long ago."

"What's that? Kill me?" Miguel took a long hard look into Alejandro's eyes, trying to decipher if what he was saying was true. But his eyes gave nothing away—as it had always been. Alejandro had been his prized creation—obedient and efficient, like a machine. But he sensed something was broken. Moving up close, he took Alejandro's hand as a lover would, interlocking his fingers to his.

"But before you kill me, Alejandro, I have one last thing to ask of you. Can you dress for me as you used to as a young boy?"

Miguel's request startled Zero. And he should have killed him without hesitation. But Miguel's touch and voice triggered an array of conflicting emotions within him—one of great love and deep hatred.

"Who said anything about killing you?" Zero finally threw back in disgust, releasing his hand from Miguel's grip.

"But I thought… then why are you here?"

"To fulfill my destiny," Zero said, staring blankly at some abstract point before him. "But for now," returning his attention to Miguel, "you are more important to me alive than dead."

"But I don't under—" Zero had pulled the gun from his suit pocket, pointing it at Miguel.

"You don't need to understand. It's time to go. Move," Zero demanded.

"I thought you never used those things."

"There's always a first. Now move." Miguel did as he was instructed.

They passed through the bedroom door, down the hallway, and stopped short at the top of the staircase. Miguel's two goons were standing at the foot of the stairway.

"Señor is everything al—" one of the goons went to ask, but quickly pulled his gun, having spotted Zero behind his master. The other followed suit.

"Drop your guns, you fools," Miguel ordered. "He does not mean to harm me. Just do as he says." The goons gave each other a questioning look but finally decided to follow Miguel's command.

"Ok, now throw your guns to the other side of the room," Zero demanded. They did as he asked.

Zero continued to move Miguel cautiously down the stairs, keeping a careful eye on the two below in case they got any last-minute ideas. Zero told Miguel's men to step aside as they reached the second last step. He then asked for the car keys. Again, they were reluctant to oblige, but Miguel ordered them to do what he said.

Zero and Miguel then resumed their walk out the door and toward the BMW SUV parked outside. Zero opened the driver's side door and got in, pointing his gun at Miguel.

"This will not end well for you, my dear Alejandro."

"I could say the same for you, Miguel," starting the car. "We'll just have to wait and see how it all goes. Until then…" but didn't finish his thought.

He noticed Miguel's men approaching, guns in hand. He put the car in drive and sped out of the driveway. In his rear-view mirror, he saw Miguel's men desperately running after the vehicle, firing freely at it. Jamming the car through the front gates, he veered right and floored the SUV down the avenue. Rechecking his rear-view mirror, Miguel's men were now mere specks on the horizon.

59

WHAT DO YOU HAVE?" I shouted, bursting through the doors once the locks were disengaged. I bypassed Moe avoiding his ceremonial hugs.

"You were right," Jimmy threw back, still at his bench, his back to me, and staring at the strange patterns on his computer screen. As I moved toward him, Moe and Samson followed the three of us, forming an arc behind Jimmy.

"So?" I asked impatiently.

"The formula that doctor gave you is the real deal," Jimmy said, turning round on his swivel chair to face me.

"You're sure?"

"See for yourself," pointing at the screen behind him.

"All I see is a headache. I have no idea what all those circles, hexes, lines, and abbreviations mean."

"I ran a series of tests numerous times, and theoretically, the vaccine will inoculate its hosts," Jimmy explained.

"Theoretically? I need to know that it works."

"Listen, if these tests work, then there's an eighty-five percent probability the vaccine will work out there as well," Jimmy explained, pointing toward an abstract point outside the room.

"I guess I've no choice but to take those odds," I said, disappointed.

"Easy, James," Moe cut in, wanting to boost my morale. "This is how it works. Any vaccine doesn't protect everyone a hundred percent. There are so many variables."

"And everyone is different," Samson pitched in.

"I get it. It's just that I'm about to play my cards with some heavy hitters, and I need to know that I'm holding an inside straight."

"It's the only play you've got, James," Jimmy added, "and I doubt anyone is holding anything close to this."

"You're right. Listen, thanks for everything you've all done."

"Hey, what are friends for," Moe said. "Come here and give me a hug." I relented to hugs from each of them. And here I thought I had gotten away with it this time around.

"Also, Samson, did you do the other thing I requested?"

"Yep," he replied, moving to his station and punching in a few keys. I followed him, with Moe and Jimmy in tow. Every time I came here, I got the feeling that hidden cameras were broadcasting our actions live on some comedy station.

"I've encrypted copies of Jimmy's findings and the doctor's formula," Samson explained. "And on your word, and only your word, I'll send them over the onion network to the proper government officials in over a hundred and ninety-five countries worldwide."

"Good. Now, which phone can I use that won't freak Moe out?"

"I rigged this one up for such an occasion," Moe said, grinning. He handed me a phone that looked just like the burner Ant had given me, but it had a few more buttons and felt heavier. I dialed the 3rd and was put through to Ant immediately.

"Cartwright. We've been expecting your call."

"Were you able to contact the President?"

"Yes. The Secretary of State, Mr. George Wilson, is here with me now. He wants to talk to you."

"Good. Put him on."

"Mr. Cartwright."

"Yes, Mr. Secretary."

"Are you on a secure line?"

"So secure that even Martian Intelligence couldn't crack it."

"I see," but obviously, he missed my pun. "Good. We're secure on our end as well. Now, were you able to secure the formula?"

"Yes, sir. But I'm told there is only an eighty-five percent probability it will work."

"Well, that's better than zero, don't you think?"

"Of course, Mr. Secretary. And have you been able to get the assurances I requested from the President?"

"Yes. It took a bit of convincing, but I explained it was the only way this would play out. So, we're in full agreement on that. I also have the document with me, which Lieutenant Ant can confirm. We can also forward a copy to you via email."

"I trust the Lieutenant. How many countries were you able to get to sign on?"

"A hundred and twenty-five so far. The usual suspects, such as Russia, North Korea and China, are holding out, but they'll come around. But that should be enough to generate a large-scale immunity."

"How long before you can get the vaccine out?" I asked.

"Well, once it's been verified, I'd say within forty-eight to seventy-two hours. We'll be getting all manufacturers capable of producing it, working on it, twenty-four-seven. They tell me that initially, they can produce around five million doses daily, but that can be ramped up to twenty mil within a week."

"That's great news," I said, feeling a sense of relief at the news.

"I must say, Mr. Cartwright, that was pretty gutsy of you to push for the vaccine to be free to everyone."

"It was the only way to guarantee that the virus could be stopped. Anything short of that would have been fruitless."

"I agree."

"Good to hear. So, if you're ready, I'll instruct the formula to be sent now."

"Let's do it."

I looked over to Samson, nodding my go-ahead. He pressed the return key and nodded back.

"It's done," I said, relaying the affirmation to the Secretary.

"When this is all over, I'd like to meet you."

"It'd be my pleasure." I lied.

I never had or planned to get involved in any political play, not that the Secretary wasn't a stand-up guy, judging by our brief conversation.

"Again, many thanks," he continued, "from me, the President and our country, hell, the whole damn world is indebted to you. If there's anything else you need, let me know."

"Thank you, sir. No, you've done enough," I said, then hung up.

"I guess you're now an American hero, James," Moe kidded.

"I'd say you guys fall more into that category. Once this is over, I plan to crawl back into the hole I came out of."

"Wise words, James," Samson offered. "That way, you won't get your head blown off like those old westerns. There's always a slick kid gunning for the top gun."

"There's still time. It's not high noon yet." Then turning to Moe, I asked, "Did you have time to look up those numbers."

"Yeah, it took a while, but I finally tracked them down. They belong to a Cessna. Manifests from a private airstrip just north of the city show the plane's scheduled to fly out this afternoon, heading to Canada."

"Great, Moe."

"So, what's next, James?" Jimmy asked.

"For you guys, nothing. Your job's done. As for me, I've got one last pesky detail to clear up."

As I reached for the door handle, Samson shouted, "Remember, James, we hold exclusive rights to your biography. And you promised we'd start work on it the next time we saw you."

"How can I forget; you mention it every time I see you."

"But you promise that same promise every time."

"I know. We'll get to it, I promise. But for now, I need to hunt down a fox."

60

GROSSE ILE MUNICIPAL AIRPORT was located on Grosse Ile, the largest of the twelve islands on the Detroit River. The residents affectionately referred to Grosse Ile as *The Island*. In '54, during the Cold War, the U.S. Army set up a base at the airport, installing Ajax-Nik missiles. The airport was one of many locations set up across the States— a last line of defense from air attacks and to protect strategic sites and cities. They removed the missiles in '63 and, by '71, transferred ownership of the airport to the township for civilian use.

The drive there took around forty-five minutes, moving from Jefferson to Grosse Ile Parkway and turning right onto Meridian. From there, I continued until I reached Groh Rd and made a right. But instead of parking in front of a sizeable glass-plated building that housed the airport's offices, I pushed a little further, taking the Groh Service Rd exit, and navigating it for a few hundred yards, until I spotted five low-lying buildings. I stopped and parked the caddy to the side, and got out.

I felt the threat of a storm moving in fast. The air felt sultry and charged by an upcoming storm front. The low-pressure system building up for days was about to break. In the distance, dark, threatening cumulonimbus clouds were gathering like a herd of bull elephants running out of space. An ominous sign. And not a great day to be flying a plane.

It took only a few minutes to reach the first hanger. Unlike the other four, this one was dome-shaped and looked like a more recent addition. As I worked my way around it, I counted fifteen spots, none of which held the aircraft I was looking for.

Samson had printed an image of the plane, including its specs. I was looking for a Cessna 172 Skyhawk. It was a single-engine, four-seater model, painted white and blue with the tail tag N46188—the same numbers Piña had overheard. It also had a cruising speed of hundred-and-forty miles per hour and a range of about seven hundred nautical miles, good enough to get Miguel to Canada.

I followed the same procedure with the subsequent three hangers as the first, but still nothing. No sign of the plane or Fox. I was now at the last hanger, the largest of the five, which I figured housed at least thirty planes. I only had another ten minutes left before Miguel's plane took off. Until now, I hadn't run into a single soul to ask if they'd seen the plane. Pilots weren't desperate enough to fly on a day like today. But my luck changed as I turned the corner of the last hangar. I found a mechanic engaged with a small floatplane in the second slot. He was working on the plane's engine. He had on a pair of oil-stained grey overalls.

"Excuse me," I said, trying to get his attention.

No response. He seemed absorbed in his work. I moved closer and realized he had on a pair of earbuds. I tapped him on the shoulder, prepared for him to swing around at the sudden intrusion and accidentally slug me with the wrench he was holding. But the opposite occurred. He pulled one of the plugs out and turned slowly to face me.

"Hi. Can I help you?"

He was of medium build, five-ten, receding hairline, and I'd put him at about forty. His face had an odd orange tint, and his lips were too thin for his large head.

"Yeah. Sorry to bother you, but I was wondering if you saw this plane around," pulling out the printout that Samson had given me. "I'm supposed to meet a friend here and fly out today but forgot which hanger number I was supposed to meet him at."

I wasn't sure if he was buying my bullshit cover story. Still, he was going along with it, giving the image a studied look.

"Not a smart move, flying out with the storm approaching," he said, stating the obvious.

"Yeah, tell me about it. But we have some urgent business in New York, and you know how it is…."

"It's your neck. Anyways. This here's a Cessna. There are about a dozen or so floating around here. Got a tailgate number?"

"I do. It's N46188."

"That's Ernie Johnson's plane."

"Where can I find it?"

"It's just next—"

The thundering sound of an engine turning over and revving up from one unit over cut him off.

"As I was about to say," now shouting. "he's next door. But it seems you're too late."

Sure enough, the Cessna I was looking for passed in front of our unit, making its way toward the airfield's runway. I figured I had two options, given the situation. Either run after it like a Looney Tunes cartoon character or commandeer a plane. I choose the former.

"Can you fly this thing?" I asked, pointing to the plane he had been working on.

"Sure. But why?"

"I need your help to catch the Cessna."

"Are you nuts? Besides, it's not my plane to use."

"It's a matter of national security." I couldn't believe I had just said that. Every Fed I'd ever met tried that line on me, and I never bought into it. And here I was, trying to pitch it for the second time in a week.

"Bullshit. What kind of security?"

"I had a hunch you wouldn't buy that line. Listen, I have no time to explain, so I apologize beforehand." I drew my colt and pointed it at his gut. "Let's go," I demanded.

He hesitated momentarily, looking down at the gun and then back at me to judge if I was being serious. I could see him working out the odds of disarming me. I guess he figured they weren't good. He closed the cover of the plane's nose and moved to the other side and into the plane's cockpit. I jumped into the passenger side. He flicked a few switches on the panel before him and flipped the ignition switch. The plane roared to life.

"Now what?" he asked, turning to me.

"Follow that damn plane."

61

THE CESSNA was a few hundred yards ahead of us. It had just taxied onto one of the three runways that formed a closed V on the field.

"Can't you make this thing go any faster?" I asked the mechanic in frustration.

"You could always get out and run," he jabbed back. "Anyway, their plane's not going anywhere until the pilot gets clearance from the tower."

"Listen, I appreciate your help?" I said, hoping to defuse the tense situation I'd created by strong-arming him.

"How do you figure? You've got a gun pointed at me. Didn't have a choice."

"The guy I'm after is in that plane," gesturing toward it, "and is behind the virus outbreak."

"No kidding? How do I know that's also not bull?"

"I couldn't make this shit up if I tried."

"Why didn't you tell me that in the first place?" glancing over, still uncertain what to make of me.

"Would you have believed me?"

"Probably not."

"How about now?"

"No. Not really," throwing me a playful grin. I figured he was warming up to me. We were now only a couple of hundred feet behind Fox's plane. The problem was it had sped up. So much for waiting for clearance.

"Damn," I blurted out.

"Easy there, partner. Don't get yourself all wound up like a porcupine caught in a desert storm."

"More like a turtle caught in a tar—"

"Hold on," he fired back, cutting me off and flipping a switch on the panel. The plane abruptly lurched forward, now throttling at full power—increasing our speed considerably. I suspected he could have done that all along but was now committed to the cause. He was getting off on the scent of the chase. We were gaining fast on the Cessna.

"So, what do you want me to do now?"

"Can you run them off the runaway?"

"What? Like they do with cars in the movies?"

"Yeah. Something like that."

"You forget a plane has wings. But let's see what I can do."

He swung the plane a hard left, pushing us up alongside the Cessna. Seeing our maneuver, one of Miguel's goons unlatched the back window of the Cessna, aiming his Uzi submachine gun in our direction. Fortunately for us, the window only opened at a forty-five-degree angle. A volley of bullets sprayed the concrete runway ahead of us, bouncing off like flies hitting a windshield. The mechanic at once pulled back, bringing us back behind the Cessna.

"Now what?" he asked, a mix of fear and adrenaline tainting his voice.

"Can't you cut them off another way?" I asked, frustrated. "There may be a way, but it's risky."

"I'm all in, but I'm not forcing you. It's your call."

Without answering, he pulled the plane's yoke toward him, causing the plane to lift, at the same time increasing the plane's acceleration. The next thing I knew, we were hovering above the Cessna. He pushed the yoke slightly forward, causing the aircraft to descend at a thirty-degree angle, two hundred feet in front of the Cessna, jamming the brakes as we hit the ground again. The Cessna had no choice but to swerve to the side to avoid slamming into us. Both planes came to a complete stop.

I jumped out, running hard toward the Cessna as Miguel and his goons exited.

Spotting my approach, the goons reached for their guns. But too late. I picked them off with a couple of precise shots. The pilot from the Cessna had also exited, raising his hands in surrender. But Miguel was another story. He started running towards the hangers.

"Not bad shooting," the mechanic offered.

"Not bad piloting," I said, returning his compliment. "Not your typical amateur pilot stuff."

"Did two stints in Afghanistan ten years back as an air force pilot. Seen and done my share of flying. Learned a few tricks," he offered back with a sly grin. "But aren't you going after your friend there?" pointing at Miguel, who had just disappeared behind one of the hangers.

"He isn't going anywhere, but yeah. If you can watch these three till the cops get here."

"Be my pleasure."

"Here, take the gun, in case they get any ideas," handing my Colt over to him.

"Won't you need it?"

"I'll improvise. It's my mark in trade."

"Be careful."

"Will do."

62

I FINALLY LOCATED Miguel between the two last hangars, bent over, hand on his chest, and breathless. My first thought was that he was having a heart attack. But he immediately erased any such possibility, straightening up to face me with a Luger in hand.

"Mr. Cartwright," he said, addressing me with a wide manic grin. "You're like a cockroach that refuses to die, no matter the means of extermination."

"I could say the same thing about you."

"Point taken. But I think we can finally put this little metaphysical drama of ours to rest," emphasizing his point by flicking his gun.

"But what about your grand scheme, your will to power?"

"We're referencing Nietzsche now. My, my, we are full of surprises. You're right, my grand plans may have fallen through, but there will be another tomorrow. You may have won the battle, my dear Cartwright, but you'll lose the war."

"How do you figure?"

"The people crave change. They need it. Things can't keep going the way they are."

"So, you and that group of misfits of yours decided you'd be the messiahs and bring about this supposed change."

"Not at all. And don't lump me in with that group or misfits as you eloquently described them. They were only a means to an end."

"What? Suppressing the birth rate so you and others could breed your kind? That's up there with mass genocide and other atrocities perpetrated throughout history. Their end game always had little to do with the progress of humanity and more to do with shoring up their feelings of superiority and a god complex."

"Perhaps there's some truth to what you say, Mr. Cartwright. But that still doesn't negate the need for change."

"So, what now? You're going to trigger a major life change for me."

"I'm sorry it has come to this. I had many chances to kill you, but I came to see you as a fellow spirit. And against my better judgment, I hoped you'd see the irrefutable logic of what I've been saying. That you'd join us in our rise to victory. But I now realize this will never happen. You'll never change. You're a dinosaur lost in the ideologies of the past. Where the world is heading, there's no place for people like yourself."

"Sorry to hear that."

"Me—"

But the Fox had no chance to finish his thought. His eyes suddenly went buggy, with an expression of disbelief flashing across his face. Then dropped dead onto the pavement below. A knife was sticking out from the back of his skull, marking his passing. The one that called himself Zero stood several feet away, looking on.

"I believe that makes us even," Zero said as he moved toward me. I, in turn, quickly retrieved Miguel's gun and pointed it squarely at his chest.

"That may be so, in terms of you saving my ass just now, but you're probably responsible for at least two other deaths I know of."

"But what's that got to do with you? They weren't friends of yours?"

"It's just this thing I have with the scales of justice. There's always a price one pays for one's choices."

"And what about you? Your hands may be clean when it comes to cold-blooded murder, but you've had your share of killing, especially those deaths caused by your meddling. What's the penalty for that?" He had a good point there. "You shouldn't be so hard on yourself, James."

"We're on a first-name basis now?"

Ignoring my question, he pushed on. "After all, these souls also made choices. Your idea of justice sounds too close to what you accused Miguel of being."

"Oh, yeah. What's that?"

"A god complex for one. None of us are in any position to pass judgment on each other. That's the folly of the justice system. Yes, we need some form of order, or we'd all kill each other off, but never for a moment do I believe that it's some infallible force that passes judgment on equal terms."

"You're quite a philosopher for a cold-blooded killer."

"Let's just say I've had much time to reflect on such matters. Besides, I'm done with all that nasty business."

"And you expect me to believe that?"

"You can believe what you want. I came to the States for two reasons."

"Which are?"

"The first part's been achieved," nodding toward Miguel's cooling corpse.

"And the other?"

"To fulfill my destiny. I've arranged a series of appointments to begin my transition. The doctor I'm seeing is one of the best in the field.

"And what transition would that be?" I asked, confused by his remark.

"That's not important. But believe me when I tell you, I will leave my previous life behind and start anew."

"I want to believe. But people don't change just like that."

I wasn't sure what to make of Zero's sudden and intimate confession, of which I had no idea what he meant exactly. But he'd been right about one thing, his take on justice. I've also felt that way—how the system lets people down. Especially the downtrodden and disadvantaged. But was he sincere about this second chance he was asking for? I was unsure, but my gut told me he was on the level.

"How do I know you're serious about this second chance?"

"You don't. But something's telling you I'm speaking the truth. Or why ask?"

"You know, sometimes you're a bit too smart for your good," I said, lowering my gun.

The bright neon lights atop the cruisers were now cutting through the dark sky. I turned to watch their approach, but only for a brief second. When I looked back, Zero was gone and nowhere to be found. He had vanished as suddenly and silently as he had appeared. The name of *Ghost* would have suited him better.

63

SIX MONTHS HAD PASSED since all hell broke. Most of the population was now vaccinated, with a small percentage still propagating conspiracy theories and refusing the vaccine. But I couldn't help feeling a sense of futility—figuring that even though we missed the bullet this time, surely there'd be another—one in which we wouldn't be so lucky.

An international warrant had been issued for Zero, but he was nowhere to be found. I assumed his transition, as he had called it, had gone according to plan.

Ant had given me a call wanting to grab breakfast at Gracie's. I figured something was on his mind, so I agreed. We both ordered one of Gracie's famous breakfast specials—three eggs, a heaping pile of bacon, hash browns and toast, plus free coffee refills. We polished it off in under ten minutes. Then Ant got to the reason for our meeting.

"So, you're still sticking to your story that you've no idea who sliced Fox's skull open."

"Officially, yes."

"It was this Zero fellow, wasn't it?"

"Could be," I said, grinning.

"When I put the fingerprints from the knife through Interpol's AFIS database, I got a hit. They belong to Alejandro Alverez, also known as Zero. He's suspected of over thirty kills that they know of."

"Not a shiny example of humanity, I must agree."

"So, why let him go?"

"Because I learned from the best. There's no such thing as black and white. There's a hell of a lot of shades of gray. And, like you once told me, it's not our place to judge. That's why there's the justice system."

"Bullshit. I don't think you believe that for a minute. There's no way you've turned over a new leaf."

"People can change," I said, not believing it myself.

"Yeah, perhaps in fairy tales and Hollywood movies. But we both know that ain't the case with this guy—even if you throw in all those shades," Ant argued. "But I do agree—we can't go around acting as judge, jury, and executioner."

"You of all people know that," hinting at his son's murder, regretting the moment I said it. Wanting to soften the blow, I quickly added, "It's tough believing in the system. There are moments where reason and justice can go to hell."

"But where would that get us—a reprieve from the pain and anger felt in the moment?" Ant countered. "You've been a cop and private investigator long enough to know that revenge doesn't solve anything. Just makes matters worse."

"Perhaps," I said, not convinced.

I saw a deep, calm understanding in Zero's face—not of a psychotic killer, but a human, demanding revenge for the unimaginable harm inflicted upon him as a child.

For him, it was the end of one lifetime and a chance to embark on another—his destiny. But how did that fit in with my so-called destiny?

I wasn't a true believer, but a more day-to-day kind of guy. Never gave any thought to tomorrow.

Perhaps it was part and parcel of the life I had chosen, with death hiding in wait at every corner. Not much of a future in that unless you believe in some higher power.

"Cartwright?" It was Ant, trying to jar me back to reality.

"Sorry. Just thinking."

"Happens to the best of us."

We both broke out in light laughter.

"Now that's a sight, seeing you two not going at each other throats." It was Gracie. She was back with a pot of coffee. "What's so funny?" she asked, refilling our cups with coffee.

"Just lack of sleep. Been up for over forty hours," I said.

"I'd say it's the coffee," Ant cut in. "You must be spiking it with something. Should get narcotics down here to check on that."

"Be all secretive, if you must, but I like the change, especially with that dreaded virus on its way out. Not only was it hurting people, but I wasn't sure how much longer I could keep this place open. Amazes me how such a tiny thing can cause such damage."

"Yeah, that vaccine seemed to show up just at the right time," Ant said, throwing a conspiratorial smile my way.

"God works in mysterious ways. And they offered the vaccine for free. What's this world coming to when corporations and governments aren't trying to bleed every penny out of you?" Gracie added.

"A better one, I hope," I offered,

"Me too," Gracie said, losing herself in thought at such a possibility. Then shaking her head, hoping to rid herself of such nonsense, left to continue her coffee rounds.

"So, what's next for you, Cartwright?" Ant asked.

"A small case came up. Off to see the client after our breakfast, then hit the sack, hopefully."

"A small case? That will be the day. Everything you touch turns to Armageddon," offering up an impish smile.

"I can't take responsibility for people's actions," I threw back. "What about you?"

"While the virus was floating around, crime came to a standstill. Can you believe it? But now that's over, they're all making up for lost time. So, it's back to the grind for yours truly."

"Interesting point you make, Ant. It seems we're incapable of saving ourselves from ourselves. It takes an outside force, a deadly one at that, to refrain us. Why's that?"

"You got me. But the way I figure, we're usually too caught up in ourselves, unable to see the big picture."

"So true," I said, agreeing. "You know, I'd rather have a natural disaster or aliens screw with us than allow some egomaniacs to dictate our fate and destroy our lives. Why do you think I demanded the vaccine be distributed for free?"

"Because you figured once the government got a hold of it, they'd be a temptation to do the same thing. Start culling the herd."

"Exactly. Perhaps not intentionally, but there'd be pressure from the corrupt higher-ups to play God."

"Well, the whole thing's behind us now. We did what we could," Ant said, looking at his watch.

"I guess it's going to be a long day for you, chasing down criminals."

"Hopefully not. I booked a day off. I just want to check out a few things at the office, then hit the sack as well."

But as if some preordained prank was being played out by an unknown jester, Ant's phone started ringing.

"Maybe not," I said.

He fished the phone from the inside suit pocket.

"Marcus, how are you?" Ant answered, relieved it wasn't the office. Marcus was one of Ant's buddies who hosted poker night every second Friday.

"Yeah, I figure I can make it," Ant said. "Cartwright? Yeah, he's around somewhere. Do I think he'll play?" Ant looked over, and I nodded in the affirmative. I figured, what the hell? I'd probably only get a few hours of sleep, anyway. There was still too much on my mind, specifically Piña.

I had gone to her arraignment to show support. Ant had also spoken with the district attorney and negotiated a deal. She ended up with three years less a day for aggravated manslaughter, which meant she'd be sent to a minimum-security facility. After that, she'd be deported. Not a great deal, but a fair one.

Ant had finished his call, and we went to pay for our breakfast. Gracie was waiting for us at the counter.

"Everything OK," she asked, again as part of her ritual, not so much about the food but our headspace. Gracie was like a stand-in mother for many who frequented her place. She cared. We told her everything was fine. Ant insisted that he pay for breakfast. When I went to protest, he said, "No big deal. I'll win it all back tonight at poker."

What Ant didn't realize was that I knew his tells, but I never exploited them, or he'd be cash poor.

"You never know, Ant. Perhaps tonight's the night destiny smiles down on me."

"I wouldn't bet on it," he said with a toying grin.

"Me neither," I countered.

As we exited onto the street, the heat of the rising sun caressed my face. It felt good. The streets were once again gridlocked with traffic, and people were scurrying here and there as if nothing had ever happened. Life as they once knew was back to normal.

If only I could become one of them. Believe in something like they did. But I knew all too well there'd always be another threat, disaster, or life crisis.

Life was like that—so precious. And it demanded only one thing. Never take it for granted.

ABOUT THE AUTHOR

OLIVER DEAN SPENCER is an international crime fiction writer and artist, who spends his time between Rome, Italy and Montreal, Canada.

To date, he's published three novels as part of the James Cartwright PI series through Original Press. He is presently working on the 4th in the Cartwright Series, *Theory of a Dead Man* and *The Fool's Overture* (Book 2 in the Devon West Mystery Series).

Spencer received his MFA in Visual Arts from the University of Ottawa (2010) and his BFA in Fine Arts from Concordia University, Montreal (2008).

When Spencer's not writing he spends his time with his daughter or playing chess at a local cafe and painting.

https://www.naccarato.org/Spencer

ORIGINAL PRESS

MYSTERY

An Original Press Mystery Publication
Montreal, Quebec, Canada